SO-AJU-451

Cattle King for a Day

A full list of L. Ron Hubbard's
novellas and short stories is provided at the back.

*Dekalogy—a group of ten volumes

L. RON HUBBARD

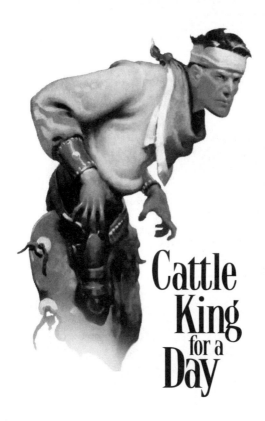

Cattle King for a Day

GALAXY
PRESS

Published by
Galaxy Press, LLC
7051 Hollywood Boulevard, Suite 200
Hollywood, CA 90028

© 2007 L. Ron Hubbard Library. All Rights Reserved.

Any unauthorized copying, translation, duplication, importation or distribution,
in whole or in part, by any means, including electronic copying, storage or
transmission, is a violation of applicable laws.

Mission Earth is a trademark owned by L. Ron Hubbard Library and
is used with permission. *Battlefield Earth* is a trademark owned
by Author Services, Inc. and is used with permission.

Horsemen illustration, Glossary illustration and *Come and Get It* story illustration
from *Western Story Magazine* are © and ™ Condé Nast Publications and are used with
their permission. Fantasy, Far-Flung Adventure and Science Fiction
illustrations: *Unknown* and *Astounding Science Fiction* copyright © by
Street & Smith Publications, Inc. Reprinted with
permission of Penny Publications, LLC.

Printed in the United States of America.

ISBN-10 1-59212-373-2
ISBN-13 978-1-59212-373-5

Library of Congress Control Number: 2007928125

Contents

Stories from Pulp Fiction's Golden Age

A ND it *was* a golden age.

The 1930s and 1940s were a vibrant, seminal time for a gigantic audience of eager readers, probably the largest per capita audience of readers in American history. The magazine racks were chock-full of publications with ragged trims, garish cover art, cheap brown pulp paper, low cover prices—and the most excitement you could hold in your hands.

"Pulp" magazines, named for their rough-cut, pulpwood paper, were a vehicle for more amazing tales than Scheherazade could have told in a million and one nights. Set apart from higher-class "slick" magazines, printed on fancy glossy paper with quality artwork and superior production values, the pulps were for the "rest of us," adventure story after adventure story for people who liked to *read*. Pulp fiction authors were no-holds-barred entertainers—real storytellers. They were more interested in a thrilling plot twist, a horrific villain or a white-knuckle adventure than they were in lavish prose or convoluted metaphors.

The sheer volume of tales released during this wondrous golden age remains unmatched in any other period of literary history—hundreds of thousands of published stories in over nine hundred different magazines. Some titles lasted only an issue or two; many magazines succumbed to paper shortages during World War II, while others endured for decades yet. Pulp fiction remains as a treasure trove of stories you can read, stories you can love, stories you can remember. The stories were driven by plot and character, with grand heroes, terrible villains, beautiful damsels (often in distress), diabolical plots, amazing places, breathless romances. The readers wanted to be taken beyond the mundane, to live adventures far removed from their ordinary lives—and the pulps rarely failed to deliver.

In that regard, pulp fiction stands in the tradition of all memorable literature. For as history has shown, good stories are much more than fancy prose. William Shakespeare, Charles Dickens, Jules Verne, Alexandre Dumas—many of the greatest literary figures wrote their fiction for the readers, not simply literary colleagues and academic admirers. And writers for pulp magazines were no exception. These publications reached an audience that dwarfed the circulations of today's short story magazines. Issues of the pulps were scooped up and read by over thirty million avid readers each month.

Because pulp fiction writers were often paid no more than a cent a word, they had to become prolific or starve. They also had to write aggressively. As Richard Kyle, publisher and editor of *Argosy*, the first and most long-lived of the pulps, so pointedly explained: "The pulp magazine writers, the best of them, worked for markets that did not write for critics or attempt to satisfy timid advertisers. Not having to answer to anyone other than their readers, they wrote about human beings on the edges of the unknown, in those new lands the future would explore. They wrote for what we would become, not for what we had already been."

Some of the more lasting names that graced the pulps include H. P. Lovecraft, Edgar Rice Burroughs, Robert E. Howard, Max Brand, Louis L'Amour, Elmore Leonard, Dashiell Hammett, Raymond Chandler, Erle Stanley Gardner, John D. MacDonald, Ray Bradbury, Isaac Asimov, Robert Heinlein—and, of course, L. Ron Hubbard.

In a word, he was among the most prolific and popular writers of the era. He was also the most enduring—hence this series—and certainly among the most legendary. It all began only months after he first tried his hand at fiction, with L. Ron Hubbard tales appearing in *Thrilling Adventures, Argosy, Five-Novels Monthly, Detective Fiction Weekly, Top-Notch, Texas Ranger, War Birds, Western Stories,* even *Romantic Range.* He could write on any subject, in any genre, from jungle explorers to deep-sea divers, from G-men and gangsters, cowboys and flying aces to mountain climbers, hard-boiled detectives and spies. But he really began to shine when he turned his talent to science fiction and fantasy of which he authored nearly fifty novels or novelettes to forever change the shape of those genres.

Following in the tradition of such famed authors as Herman Melville, Mark Twain, Jack London and Ernest Hemingway, Ron Hubbard actually lived adventures that his own characters would have admired—as an ethnologist among primitive tribes, as prospector and engineer in hostile climes, as a captain of vessels on four oceans. He even wrote a series of articles for *Argosy,* called "Hell Job," in which he lived and told of the most dangerous professions a man could put his hand to.

Finally, and just for good measure, he was also an accomplished photographer, artist, filmmaker, musician and educator. But he was first and foremost a *writer,* and that's the L. Ron Hubbard we come to know through the pages of this volume.

This library of Stories from the Golden Age presents the best of L. Ron Hubbard's fiction from the heyday of storytelling, the Golden Age of the pulp magazines. In these eighty volumes, readers are treated to a full banquet of 153 stories, a kaleidoscope of tales representing every imaginable genre: science fiction, fantasy, western, mystery, thriller, horror, even romance—action of all kinds and in all places.

Because the pulps themselves were printed on such inexpensive paper with high acid content, issues were not meant to endure. As the years go by, the original issues of every pulp from *Argosy* through *Zeppelin Stories* continue crumbling into brittle, brown dust. This library preserves the L. Ron Hubbard tales from that era, presented with a distinctive look that brings back the nostalgic flavor of those times.

L. Ron Hubbard's Stories from the Golden Age has something for every taste, every reader. These tales will return you to a time when fiction was good clean entertainment and the most fun a kid could have on a rainy afternoon or the best thing an adult could enjoy after a long day at work.

Pick up a volume, and remember what reading is supposed to be all about. Remember curling up with a *great story.*

—Kevin J. Anderson

KEVIN J. ANDERSON *is the author of more than ninety critically acclaimed works of speculative fiction, including The Saga of Seven Suns, the continuation of the Dune Chronicles with Brian Herbert, and his* New York Times *bestselling novelization of L. Ron Hubbard's* Ai! Pedrito!

Cattle King for a Day

Chapter One

CHINOOK SHANNON was new to Montana. He did not know the simple courtesies connected with meeting road agents. In fact, he did not even know the term, being from Arizony where road agents are just plain bandits.

All Chinook Shannon knew was that the three men who had so suddenly leaped out in the trail before him meant no good to either his person or his property.

As far as the person went, Chinook was rich, being young and range-toughened and well proportioned. He had his health, a good gun eye and a fine set of teeth.

But as to property, he was somewhat beggared. His gear was battered after the two months' hard ride from Arizony to Montana. His batwings were scarred, his boots had run-over heels and his spurs were dull. His hat was floppy with rain and wind and his checkered shirt was just entering its third week unwashed.

And so it was that Chinook Shannon felt little worried about these three gentlemen.

He had come out of a creek bed and up the slope toward two huge boulders. A sudden movement had caused him to rein in. Three riders, more or less weathered and definitely tougher than bear steak, had swung into the trail.

It was impossible to get by. Chinook crooked a heel around his applehorn, extracted a sack of Bull and built himself a smoke, keeping his eye upon the three holstered guns without seeming the least bit worried.

The man in the lead had a complexion like fat meat and the afternoon sun of the mountain fall was melting him drop by drop. Only his gun showed any care and that glittered, polished with long and frequent usage.

"You're a stranger," decided the gentleman in the lead.

"Yep," said Chinook, lighting up as casually as possible.

"From desert country, judging the rig."

"Yep," replied Chinook.

"And you come a long ways fast."

"Hundred percent so far. Long as we're telling fortunes, will I marry a blonde or brunette?"

"Neither," said the man in the lead. "You ain't going to live that long if you keep on up this trail."

"If I'm not mistaken," said Chinook, "this is the public thoroughfare to Bull Butte."

"You ain't going to Bull Butte."

"Now, I wouldn't say that," replied Chinook, easily.

"You're going to turn around and head south again or else."

"Else what?"

"Else we'll cave a bank in on you, that's what."

"Think there's enough of you to do that?"

"Plenty," said the leader.

"Sure you haven't got my identity tangled with somebody else?" said Chinook.

"Nope. According to a pal in Cheyenne, you're Chinook Shannon."

"Pleased to meet *you*," said Chinook.

"Yeah, I'm Jake Humphrey. Brad Kendall says you ain't going to arrive in Bull Butte."

"He's wrong," said Chinook, "but thanks for the trouble. And thanks for the name."

"What name?" snapped Humphrey.

"Brad Kendall's name. I was the least bit hazy who to look for." Chinook set his toe back in the stirrup, took a long puff on the cigarette, flipped it down toward the stream and gave every appearance of a man about to ride straight ahead.

Jake Humphrey's two men kept their ground.

"I wouldn't want you to get hurt," said Humphrey. "But . . ." His hand ripped inside his coat and steel flashed as his short gun came out.

Chinook dug spur. His horse, Wild Cat, reared. Chinook's Peacemaker spewed thunder, flame and lead.

Humphrey's short gun leaped sideways and into the brush. The three horses before Chinook tangled up.

Cursing, trying to get at their holsters, Humphrey's two lieutenants were almost thrown by the plunging Wild Cat's rush between them.

Chinook crouched low over Wild Cat's mane. A .44 screamed between Wild Cat's blurred forelegs. Chinook careened around a turn in the wooded trail, plunged off at right angles on a less distinct path and raced ahead under the low branches which whipped unmercifully at him.

He came into a dry gulch, turned down it, scrambled up the side, darted into another patch of woods and reined in.

He could hear the far-off shouts of the three reception committee members and knew that they were trying to track him over the stony paths.

At a canter, Chinook continued toward Bull Butte, choosing his own way, very puzzled as to the meeting and just why a man named Brad Kendall should desire his untimely demise.

"Very strange," he told Wild Cat. "Maybe Mr. Borden can clear it all up for me."

With that in mind, he entered the thriving town of Bull Butte. The metropolis consisted of two slovenly rows of weathered false-front buildings, a sign which said "Post Office, Bull Butte, Montana" and another sign which said "The Diamond Palace."

At one end of the hoof-pulverized street was a squat, fortlike affair, quite obviously the bank.

Chinook swung off, hitched Wild Cat to the rack, brushed hopelessly at the white dust which covered both of them and then, with jingle bobs tinglinging and leather creaking, he entered the heavy door.

The bank was rather well built. The cashier had iron bars before him, perhaps as a reminder of what would happen if he tampered with the funds, and a Derringer beside the till. There was a swinging gate and a sign which said "Paul Borden, President."

Without waiting for an invitation, Chinook pushed through, tilted his hat to the back of his blond head, hooked his thumbs in his cartridge belt and said, "Howdy."

Banker Borden looked up. No sign of recognition could be detected on his ruddy, soft face. Somewhat annoyed at the intrusion, he said briskly, "You wish to see me about some business?"

"Yep," said Chinook.

"I don't seem to place you. One of Kendall's men?"

"Nope."

"Well, then," said Banker Borden, exasperated, "where are you from?"

"Arizony."

Borden paled slightly. He had half risen from his chair. He sank back now, shakily, removed his glasses, polished them and looked fixedly at Chinook. He saw a sight which did not at all encourage him. He saw six feet two of range rider encased in batwings, vest and flat-brimmed hat. He saw the white dust of travel and the weary lines on Chinook's young face. He saw the way the ivory-butted, silver-chased Peacemaker was lashed down low on Chinook's thigh and an empty loop in the cartridge belt.

"You're . . . you're Chinook Shannon."

"Yep."

"And . . . and you've come to see about the Slash S ranch."

"Yep."

"But . . . but I wired you about your grandfather's death two months ago."

"Yep."

"See here, Shannon," wailed the banker, "you can't keep a man in suspense like that for two months and then suddenly turn up. You know something had to be done about the Slash S."

"Yep. I'm going to do it."

"Why . . . why, yes, of course, Shannon."

"Of course," said Chinook. "I believe you said my grandfather died?"

"Uh . . . well, that's right."

"Murdered, perhaps?"

"Why, no! What makes you think that?"

"Shannons ain't like other people. They don't die natural deaths. I believe I'm the heir."

"Yes . . . yes, the sole heir to the Slash S."

"I believe," said Chinook, "that it's the biggest spread east of the mountains."

"Well . . . er . . . yes."

"There were, the last time my grandad wrote, about four thousand head of good beef cattle there, which he was to ship in the fall. Did he ship?"

"Well . . . no . . . that is . . . His death was a very great shock to all of us, Mr. Shannon. I think the country sustained a great loss. . . ."

"Why didn't he ship?"

"Well . . . er . . . perhaps I had better start at the beginning, Mr. Shannon. You, I believe, were about to come north anyway to take over your grandfather's ranch and run it for him. He said as much."

"He figured he was getting old," volunteered Chinook. "Me, I've always been a drifter and I always wanted to be one of those things they call a cattle king. Now, you savvy?"

"Well . . . yes . . . of course. Your grandfather was very fond of you, I believe."

"Down Texas way, when I was a little shaver. Yes. Now come on. What happened to the shipment? Train wreck, rustling, what?"

Borden squirmed and looked beadily at Chinook's Peacemaker. Taking a long breath, he plunged.

"There's been some trouble, Mr. Shannon. Montana is divided into three lines of endeavor: sheep, cattle and mining. Sometimes, Mr. Shannon, those three come into conflict. In this instance, it was cattle and mining."

"Go on," said Chinook.

"The Shoshone Mining Company discovered a rich lode up Pan Creek, a stream of water which bisects the Slash S. Properly speaking, Mr. Shannon, the ground did not exactly belong to your grandfather, but the water below that did."

"Go on," said Chinook.

"Now you are not a mining man, Mr. Shannon, but you must understand that minerals have the upper hand over mere cattle land. And you must understand that the wealth of this state depends upon gold mining at the moment. You have heard of cyanide mining?"

"Nope," said Chinook.

"It is a process lately introduced into Montana. Cyanide is utilized to remove the gold content from the crushed ore. Unfortunately for your grandfather's ranch, a great deal of this cyanide was swept away by the stream known as Pan Creek and was carried down into the watering pools. Cyanide, Mr. Shannon, is extremely poisonous. The cattle, Mr. Shannon, are dead."

"Four thousand head?"

"I regret to say," said Banker Borden, his eyes on the gun.

"Well, but there's a chance to get more stock and to stop the spilling of this stuff into Pan Creek," said Chinook.

"My bank," said Borden, "most unfortunately holds paper on the Slash S to the amount of twenty-six thousand dollars."

"Well, we'll fix that somehow. I want to roam around a little. I got an idea, Borden, that this ain't exactly fifty-two cards in the deck."

"Young man, do you mean to implicate—"

"Yep."

"Well, I . . . that is . . . er . . . I must inform you that I mean to foreclose at noon tomorrow. The sheriff has already issued the papers."

"No chance that you might grant an extension?"

"Business is business," said Borden.

"You can call it by that name," replied Chinook. "It's almost noon now. You mean to say that for twenty-four hours, I am the owner of the Slash S?"

"I have already probated awaiting your signature, but I hardly think that it is worth your while, unless you have twenty-six thousand dollars on your person."

"Give me your pen." Chinook turned the legal document around, looked it over, and saw that it looked all right. He signed.

"I think," said Borden, "that you are being very foolish. Twenty-four hours is very little time, and I would suggest—"

"Suggest anything you want," said Chinook, buttoning a copy into his batwing pocket. "But wait until I've got a little more time."

He walked out.

Chapter Two

BULL BUTTE, at midday, seemed to be populated principally with four dogs which were bent upon a lawless looting of the general store's garbage dump.

Except for these, Chinook saw only the weathered buildings and, of course, his horse, Wild Cat. Finding no one at home in the livery stable, Chinook took the liberty of bedding and feeding his worthy mount, and when that was completed he walked through the dusky, dusty building toward the front door.

If rattlesnakes could talk, their voices would probably have resembled that which came from the shadows of a stall.

"Goin' someplace, Shannon?"

Chinook did not make a sudden movement. He stopped and leaned against a two-by-four and looked steadily in front of him.

Two clicks followed, of a lethal quality peculiar to a Colt hog leg. A boot scuffed board. The voice's owner stepped into Chinook's view.

He was squat, as though some enormous weight had hit him on top of the head and battered him down. His brow was low and almost covered with black eyebrows. His eyes were snaky and small. His nose flared into enormous, hairy nostrils above a lipless grin.

"I'm Kendall, Shannon. I'm Brad Kendall, and there ain't a tougher gent west of the Mississippi, see? I'm poison. You heard of me."

"Sure," said Chinook. "Sure I heard of you. That mare back there just now described you perfectly."

Kendall juggled his gun and his grin broadened. Suddenly he understood what Chinook meant and he lurched forward, hand tightening on the butt.

"You're one of these smart Southerners, are you? One of these fast-draw, hell-on-wheels Texas boys, are you? You come up here maybe to show us a few things?"

"I did," said Chinook.

"I bet your mama don't know you're out. How come my boys didn't stop you? Never mind, shuck that belt and we'll get going."

"I'm staying where I am, Kendall."

"Huh! Well, what the hell, it don't make no difference where I get you. I just wanted you to know what happens to gents that come snooping around, that's all. You got a nerve with you, sonny. You know I got twenty guns that says I'm right, and more than that, I got me. What I do in this country is the law. One Shannon's already been convinced and here's where I convince—"

As he spoke, his finger was tightening and the muzzle was gradually coming to a sight on Chinook's heart. Chinook tried to think of something. If he stepped aside and drew, he would still be too late. There was no way to beat the hammer.

Another voice whined, "What the hell you up to, Kendall?"

Kendall whirled and stared at a short, bowlegged oldster

who stood just inside the livery stable door. Kendall glared at the newcomer's gun and lowered his own into his holster. There was nothing else he could do.

Across the street the swinging doors of the Diamond Palace jumped outward. Two hard-looking riders strode down the steps and started to cross the street.

Chinook did not have to be told that these two were part of Kendall's outfit. Somehow, all of Kendall's men were of a similar stamp.

Chinook flipped Kendall's hog leg out and into a pile of straw. The oldster scurried into the dimness, still covering Kendall.

"Come on," said the bowlegged one to Chinook. "Don't stand there gawping. We've got to get the hell out of here before them two arrive."

Led hurriedly out through the rear of the building, Chinook had no time to speculate upon his savior's identity and the oldster seemed to take it as a matter of course that Chinook knew.

They skirted the back of the livery stable, walking over piles of rubbish and, at the bowlegged one's request, entered another smaller shack which had barred windows.

A man with a big nose and flabby jowls looked up from a newspaper, over his upraised boot toes and at the two callers. A large star was prominent upon his chest.

"Hello, Deke," said the sheriff. "Who's your friend?"

"He's Chinook Shannon. Can't you tell it? You always was blind in one eye. You got to give him a hand. Kendall was just trying to knock him off over in the barn."

"My, my," said the sheriff, rubbing his nose and looking apprehensively at the door. "Er . . . aw . . . do you suppose they know he came in here, Deke?"

"No, they think maybe he rode away. Shannon, in spite of that jackrabbit expression on his face, this is Sheriff Taggart. Your grandpappy put him in office."

Chinook shook Taggart's flabby, wet hand.

"In case your grandpappy never mentioned me to you, I'm Deacon Murphy, his foreman."

"Pleased to meet you," said Chinook. "Now that we're all properly introduced, let me inquire about this Kendall. How come he's running Bull Butte?"

"Took it over this spring," said Deke. "The son of a jackass took over a mine up Pan Creek, poisoned all our stock with cyanide and raised hell in general. Damn him, he didn't fight square. He murdered your grandpappy and then went over the rest of us like a prairie fire. The boys scattered to hell and gone but I've hung around Bull Butte for two months waiting for you to come. And now that you're here, you've only got the place for a day and we can't do anything in that length of time."

"How about the courts?" said Chinook.

"Er . . . aw . . . ahumph," said Taggart. "When the circuit judge came . . . er . . . Deke Murphy was the only witness that could be got—"

"Because you was scared to testify," snapped Deke, rubbing emphatically at his gray whiskers. "But what you going to do, son?"

"Murphy," said Shannon, "the least I can do is nail the man that shot my grandfather."

"Kendall," said Deke.

"And I can at least make a try to save the Slash S."

"Borden's got his bug eye on it," said Deke.

"I know. I've talked to him. Murphy, all my life I've wanted to be what they call a cattle king. I've drifted around and I've never really amounted to much. Well, I'm one now, if only for twenty-four hours. Sheriff, if I shoot it out with this crowd, where do I stand with you?"

"Well . . . aw . . . er . . . ahumph . . . aw . . . that is, if you were to get all of them, Shannon, *all of them*, I think you would find me quite agreeable. But I . . . er . . . aw . . . cannot countenance any slaughter which would . . . aw . . . fail to clean out them *all*. You are, after all, Shannon, but one man and they are twenty-one. I am afraid . . ."

"You don't have to tell him how scared you are," snapped Deke. "If we get them all, is it to be an even break in the eyes of the law?"

"An uneven break," said Taggart, "if you should ask me. I am afraid, Deke, that this young man is committing suicide—"

"That's my lookout," said Chinook. "First, Murphy, we'd better look over the Slash S and that mine. Sheriff, you'll please give us a hand in getting our horses?"

"Not me," said Taggart, definitely.

"Then you cover me, Murphy," said Chinook. "Daylight's burning."

Chapter Three

C HINOOK SHANNON and Deke Murphy got out of Bull Butte with very great caution. It was no part of their plan to get killed, and at their moment of departure, Kendall and his outfit were combing the town with just that idea in mind.

However, Kendall forgot about the sheriff's office, simply because almost everybody forgot about Taggart.

Slipping the horses and gear out of the back of the livery stable, Chinook led off immediately into the brush behind the sheriff's office where he was joined by Deke.

They saddled and rode circuitously in the direction of the Slash S, some five miles from Bull Butte.

They pulled up on the rim of a butte and Deke made an expansive motion with his hand.

"There," said Deke, "is the Shannon domain. Everything you can see from here is yours."

Chinook shaded his eyes with his hat and stared far out across the wide plains. The ranch houses were a small, deserted patch of weathered boards with windows like sightless eyes. The corrals were empty, doors stood open at the mercy of the wind.

Through the middle of the vast plain a stream wandered,

flanked by willows and alder, and even from the butte, Chinook could see the whiteness of the water.

The prairie was dotted with scraps of hide, skulls and scattered bones, the remnants of a once mighty herd, now dead and left to blend with the buffalo grass.

A meadowlark whistled somewhere near at hand. The lonely wind stirred in the sage. A coyote slunk out of a coulee and disappeared behind the buildings.

It was a saddening, desolate scene, a sorry domain no matter how large and how fertile.

"We buried your grandad on that knoll behind the house. Do you want to go down there?"

"No," said Chinook, hitching his Peacemaker up on his thigh. "I'll go there tomorrow when I can tell him that it's done." He looked away from Deke and in a muffled voice added, "Where's that goddamned mine?"

They rode north for a little more than three miles and came out on a bluff. Chinook dismounted away from the rim, pulled a small telescope from his saddlebag and approached the edge.

The mine was in a canyon. A stamp mill was banging harshly, grinding quartz to dust. Men were moving about the vats, in and out of the drifts and among the shacks. They were all armed.

The telescope told Chinook that the place was impregnable. A red-shirted guard sat at each end of the canyon. Kendall was taking no chances of retaliation.

"Pretty complete layout," said Chinook.

"They freighted in from the Missouri," said Deke.

The telescope told Chinook that the place was impregnable.
A red-shirted guard sat at each end of the canyon. Kendall
was taking no chances of retaliation.

"They must have taken out a lot of gold."

"I dunno. They ship it every stage and the express box is always nice and heavy. Kendall ain't likely to let this slip out of his hands. Come to think of it, there'll be a stage through Bull Butte tonight."

"Uh-huh," said Chinook. "By the way, how often does that stage go through?"

"Twice a week. Why?"

"That isn't so good." Chinook turned his glass on the mine again and presently said, "Wells Fargo Express?"

"Naw. This is too far out of the way for anything but a private feeder."

"Good. How do they ship their ingots?"

"Why, by the bank, I guess. I never noticed. What you got in mind, Shannon?"

"Nothing definite. It's a cinch two men wouldn't stand a chance storming that mine. Suicide. And Kendall's got too many guns around him all the time . . . and besides, killing Kendall won't straighten out everything."

"Maybe I should have shot him today," said Deke, thoughtfully rubbing his whiskers. "But I dunno. I kind of got upset when his two gunslingers came out of the saloon looking for him. I ain't so much with a hog leg."

"Can't even load one, I'll bet."

"Well . . . But you gotta admit I figured those two gunslingers would blast us down if they so much as heard a hammer click."

"Never mind," said Chinook, consolingly. "Killing Kendall

is a last resort. The first thing I've got to do is pay up to the bank."

"You really think you can find twenty-six thousand dollars?"

Chinook gave Deke a sad grin. "I don't really think so, but damn it, Deke Murphy, me and Wild Cat rode all the way from Arizony to Montana to settle up a score, and just because we arrived twenty-four hours before the hammer dropped isn't any reason to quit trying. I've got ideas and my ideas lead me to Bull Butte." Chinook closed up his small telescope and slid back away from the rim, scowling thoughtfully.

"How is it," said Chinook, "that this claim was right here all the time and nobody knew it until Kendall came along?"

"Hell, we knew about it. Everybody knew about it. But we're in the cattle business. We didn't know nothing about mines. Your grandpappy knew about it when he patched this range together. Old guy by the name of Stewart was here long before we was. Used to live up here at the mine. He'd pan some below it and sink his shaft a little deeper, but he never made much on it. Leastways, judging how he used to weasel grub out of your grandpappy. Grub and tobacco. He was right glad to have company, Stewart was. He'd been here in these hills for years. He'd lived right here for seven. Great old guy. Lots of wild Indian yarns, plenty of Indian ways. Begged off your grandpappy all the time. Last winter old Stewart died and right afterwards this Kendall appeared and started in to work the diggings. Your grandpappy was going to do something legal about it, if I remember, but . . . well, they shot him before he had a chance."

21

"That doubles it."

"Doubles what?" said Deke.

"My reason for going to Bull Butte tonight."

"I wouldn't show myself. Kendall's hellbent on ventilating you considerable."

"I don't doubt it," said Chinook. "Now I see the extent of these workings. Let's go someplace where I can get something to eat. Thinking always did give me a powerful appetite."

Chapter Four

AFTER six o'clock, it was Bull Butte's custom to get noisy. In the past the long-departed Slash S crew had amused themselves by shooting at sheepherders, windows, lamps and mirrors. At present the Shoshone mining men held full sway. Trained in the noble art of self-defense and anxious to keep in practice, the imported gunslingers were accustomed to brawl among themselves.

But tonight was different. Laughter in Bull Butte had a higher pitched, metallic ring and, when heard from afar, it resembled closely the baying of a hound pack.

Guns were loose in the town this night.

A target for ready lead was somewhere in the vicinity and the Shoshone men were already spending on credit the bounty offered for a certain blond scalp.

It did not occur to those hard pill-throwers that Kendall must be mighty worried to put a five-thousand dollar price on the head of one man. The way Kendall put it, the reward was something like a poker stake, a chance to break the monotony and to reward some worthy killer.

Chinook, the quarry, tied his horse, Wild Cat, in a small clearing some distance from town, loosened the cinch and made sure of the grass.

Deke Murphy stood in the shadows watching. In spite of a

long fighting life, Deke could not be very easy about Chinook's necessarily sketchy plans. Chinook would have to take terrific chances to win and the odds, thought Deke, were something like a thousand to one against Chinook's paying Borden, about five thousand to one against Chinook's killing Kendall, about ten thousand to one against retrieving the Slash S range from the effects of the Shoshone mine. Chinook's chances of getting into Bull Butte and back again alive were fairly good, only about a hundred to one.

Chinook removed the jingle bobs from his spurs, covered the bright silver ring which held his bonnet strings, loosened his Peacemaker, and gave Deke a half salute.

"I'll be back in a half-hour," said Chinook. "Wait for me unless you hear a whole lot of gunfire."

Deke nodded dumbly.

Chinook picked his way through the dark trees toward the squares of yellow light which marked Bull Butte's main thoroughfare.

As he approached, the noise grew louder and the lights brighter. Men were walking up and down the high boardwalk and when they passed windows, light flashed on brass and steel.

Chinook stood for some time in the shadow of a wall, looking across the light and dark patchwork of the street at the Diamond Palace Saloon. Kendall was not in evidence and only nine or ten of his men could be seen.

As Chinook knew that nothing had been brought down from the mine to Bull Butte that afternoon, intelligence gained by hours of watching, he expected the shipment to arrive that night.

The stage was not yet there. It would arrive, according to Deke, in about two hours and would depart after a short stop. It had to make a hundred-and-fifteen-mile run from dawn to dawn on an extremely bad road with only two relays.

Chinook did not have long to wait.

Kendall rode into the light at the other end of the street, looking like a barrel tied to a saddle. Behind him were six men, strung on either side of a pack horse. The black muzzles of rifles jutted out from the crooks of their arms.

The midweek take of the Shoshone mine had arrived.

One of the gunmen yelled at a friend up on the boardwalk that he would be setting them up in a few minutes. Kendall stared shiftily into the shadows between the buildings. Chinook drew back out of sight.

The horses stopped in front of the bank. Lamplight flooded the building's hitch rack and walk. Borden came out.

"You're just in time, Mr. Kendall," said Borden. "I was getting worried."

"Aw, he's been jumping at shadows," said Jake Humphrey at Kendall's right.

"You ain't seen anything of that young fool, have you, Borden?" said Kendall.

"Why, just before noon he—"

"I know. I know. I mean tonight."

"I wouldn't carry things too far, Kendall," said Borden. "After all, you've got twenty of the hardest fighters this side of Dodge, and one man . . ."

"One bullet can do a hell of a lot of damage," said Kendall. "Aw, don't get me wrong. Maybe you think I'm scared of the

25

rat. I'm not. I'm just anxious to plug him and get it over with. I don't want any trouble. Not with the Shoshone running like she is."

"Good, eh?" said Borden.

"Unload her, Jake, and show him."

Jake and another man dragged the pack off the horse and, with some effort, carried it inside the bank. Presently Chinook heard a vault door clang shut.

Kendall and his men came out.

"You, Steve," said Kendall. "And you, Lippy. Stay here and keep your eyes open."

"That scalp money go for us?" said the man addressed as Lippy.

"It does," said Kendall, walking toward the Diamond Palace with the other four.

Chinook waited for ten minutes or more. The racket in the saloon steadied down to a monotonous din. Kendall did not appear again.

Chinook surveyed the street again. On the other side of the sheriff's office he saw a light and knew that Taggart was at home. A wicked grin pushed the tightness away from his mouth. He shoved his hat back a little as he always did when he contemplated brashness. A quick survey of the street showed him that the way was clear.

He scouted through the brush and came up behind the office, wading through the masses of tin cans as quietly as possible.

He knocked gently upon the sheriff's back door.

Taggart's semibald head appeared at the back window.

Boots scuffed inside. The door let out a widening crack of light and there was Taggart, a scatter-gun clutched nervously to his heaving chest.

"It . . . er . . . aw . . . Shannon!" gulped Taggart, fumbling with his weapon. "You . . . ahumph . . . Go away!"

"I've got business," said Chinook. "And if I should happen to come out on top of this heap, Sheriff, my memory will be pretty long."

"Eh . . . er . . . ah . . . Come in, come in, Mr. Shannon." Taggart looked forlornly at his scatter-gun, realized that it was pointing at Chinook's checkered chest and quickly propped it in a corner.

Chinook entered and closed the door. He drew down the blind and shut off the outer office. He sat down at a table cluttered with dirty plates and pans and built himself a smoke.

Taggart nervously massaged his red-veined, bulbous nose and darted a glance in the direction of the noisy street as though he could see through both inner and outer walls.

"Taggart," said Chinook. "My grandfather had more kindness than judgment, sometimes."

"Er . . . aw . . . yes, yes. A fine man, your grandfather. Gentleman of the old school. Splendid fellow." Taggart wiggled with anxiety. "You . . . er . . . aw . . . have some business with me?"

"Yes. The circuit court stops here occasionally, at least when there's business to be done. Their records, or at least a schedule of business, a docket, should be in your possession. Give, Taggart."

"Why . . . aw . . . ahumph . . . I believe . . ."

"Give," said Chinook.

Taggart shuffled into the outer office and Chinook heard a safe door open and shut. Taggart came back laden with ledgers.

"I am sure . . . that is, I might suggest . . . er . . . aw . . . aw . . . that you will probably find nothing there, Mr. Shannon."

Chinook was paying no attention to him. He swept back the smeared plates and stacked up the books. Starting with the top he went along their backs with his finger. Finally, he found the one he wanted. Spreading it open, he rapidly rattled through the pages.

Presently Taggart was blasted down with a glare. "Taggart," said Chinook. "You have been negligent in your duties. This entry states in so many words that the circuit court, at the request of my grandfather, placed a restraining injunction against the Shoshone Mining Company pending investigation of all titles, water rights, patents and claims. It further states that the Shoshone Mining Company may continue to operate only insofar as minerals mined be placed in escrow pending the further findings of this court. You served that injunction?"

"Well . . . now . . . to be frank, Mr. Shannon . . . I . . . er . . . aw . . . Your grandfather was murdered and I was . . . that is . . . er . . . so taken up with the investigation of his death that . . . ahem . . . the . . . ahumph . . . matter quite slipped my mind."

"I suppose so," said Chinook. "And as there was no further complaint from this region, the circuit court has not been back since. Look here! Here's the injunction in an envelope all ready for the serving, signed by the judge, to be handed personally to Brad Kendall and operating from the date of issue. Taggart, we must be firm."

"Oh, of course, of course. Quite right. Yes, yes, yes indeed, Mr. Shannon."

"I did not think that my grandfather would let this matter rest without a fight. Whether you know it or not, Taggart, there is a law, a Federal law, about water. The Mining Act of 1872, Title Thirty-two, Chapter Six, Revised Statutes, Article Two Thousand Three Hundred and Thirty-nine, specifically states that '. . . whenever any person, in the construction of a ditch or canal, injures or damages the possession of any settler on the public domain, the party committing such injury or damage shall be liable to the party injured for such injury and damage.' It further states, Taggart, 'that such prior rights to water shall be protected in their vested rights and that the matter is within the province of a court.'"

"Aw . . . aw . . . aw . . . My, my, Mr. Shannon, I did not know that you were a lawyer."

Chinook omitted telling him that he had just then read the matter straight off the record. Chinook growled, "There's a lot of things you don't know, Taggart, and one of them is that you are going to serve this injunction."

"Of course . . . of course, Mr. Shannon. I . . . er . . . ahumph . . . however, must act, unfortunately, on the morrow in the foreclosure of the . . . well . . . er . . . the Slash S. You understand, Mr. Shannon, that the papers are already in Borden's hands and I . . . er . . . aw . . . must go through with the formality."

"I understand all that. But you are going to serve this injunction within the next five minutes."

"Ah . . . I'm WHAT?"

"You're going to walk into your office, open the door and send the first man who passes, for Kendall. I will be standing right behind this door, looking through the keyhole with the muzzle of my gun accurately centered upon the middle of your flabby spine. One motion extra or one too many blinks or gulps and I'll plug you first, Kendall second, and then I'll take his men with your scatter-gun as they rush in. On your horse, Sheriff."

Taggart developed an alarming case of palsy. Beads of sweat as big as buttons gleamed on his forehead, broke and cascaded in torrents down his face. Everything except the tip of his nose went gray. His nose turned lavender. His eyeballs jiggled up and down, matching the vibration tempo of his Adam's apple.

Chinook flipped his Peacemaker out of his holster, tossed it up in a spin, caught it cocked.

But the neatness of the pinwheel was lost upon Taggart. He only saw that the gun's muzzle was suddenly increased to the size of a Sioux shield.

Taggart tried to protest. He dropped to his knees and whined. He groveled and whimpered. Chinook began to count slowly.

As Taggart did not know what number Chinook was trying to arrive at before he shot, he yelped in terror, flung into his outer office, shoved his face outside the front door and spotted a passing Kendall gunman.

"S-S-S-Send K-K-K-Kendall over here a s-s-s-second."

The gunman went away. Taggart crept back for the envelope and the injunction. Chinook handed it out, closed the door and knelt at the keyhole.

Kendall came in a few minutes. He was thick and tipsy with rotgut whiskey.

Kendall missed Taggart's pallor, or possibly attributed it to the terror of the Kendall name.

"What the hell's eating you, moss-face?" said Kendall.

"I-I g-g-g-g-got a l-l-l-letter I b-b-been meaning to give you," wailed Taggart, quickly thrusting the paper into Kendall's hand as though it was on fire.

Kendall grunted and opened it. He read it three times and then, gradually, its contents began to sink in.

"Goddamn you for a blundering fool!" volleyed Kendall, wide nostrils quivering, black teeth biting off the tails of the words. "What in the name of ——"

It was all unquotable. It treated Taggart's family tree from its inception, followed through several score generations, caught up with Taggart's personal appearance, filthy habits, general demeanor, and went on to revile Taggart's posterity.

Rage dulled Kendall's wits. Otherwise he might have guessed what lay on the other side of that door. He did not. He put a comma to his phrases by tearing the injunction into small pieces, one at a time, and hurling them into Taggart's face.

With the injunction gone, Kendall promised lengthy vengeance, slow torture, expressed a wish to minutely examine Taggart's abdomen with a sharp knife, and finally went away still roaring, having knocked Taggart and Taggart's desk into a hash of bruises and splinters.

Taggart closed the door, limped into the back room, moaning and whining.

Chinook solemnly thanked him and then, just as solemnly, said, "And now about a star."

"A star?" whispered Taggart, too weak from shock to talk out loud.

"Sure," said Chinook. "You got authority to swear in deputies. You're swearing me in as a deputy sheriff right now."

"It . . . er . . . won't do you any good," gulped Taggart. "You . . . you'll be dead before morning. You . . . you heard what he said. I'll be dead and you'll be dead . . . oh, why did you ever have to come into this country?"

"The star," insisted Chinook.

Taggart's resistance was gone. Protesting only with great feebleness, he fished a rusty badge out of his dresser, limply handed it to Chinook, muttered some words which Chinook took to be an administered oath, and then, with terrific suddenness, Taggart collapsed in a chair and fumbled blindly for a whiskey bottle.

"Thanks again, Sheriff," said Chinook. "I knew my grandfather's choice would know how to do his duty like a man."

"You . . . you think so?" gasped Taggart, surprised.

"I do. See you at the funeral."

"W-What funeral?"

"I dunno, just yet, but I'll see you there. Good night."

Chapter Five

A T ten o'clock, about an hour after the stage had left Bull Butte, Bear Paw Canyon was filled with the clatter of hoofs, the jingle of chain, and the groan and creak of ungreased springs.

The four horses toiled through the dark, their backs shining faintly under the yellow gleam of the two coach lamps just under the box. Ahead the rough wagon trail was gray in the starlight, winding up the side of the wooded slope.

Chinook watched it come with immense satisfaction. He drew his Peacemaker and stepped away from Wild Cat and up on an overhanging boulder.

Across the road, with Sheriff Taggart's double-bitted ax sticking upright on it, lay an expertly felled pine. The stage could not go up the steep bank, nor could it move around on the left because of the trees. The stage, as there was not room for a turn, would have to stop.

Chinook crouched, waiting.

The hoofbeats of the trotting four came nearer. Chinook could see a messenger half-asleep beside the driver. The driver, with one foot resting lightly on the brake, chin sunk in his collar, made a dejected black silhouette in the upflash of the lamps.

Abruptly the lead horse stopped. His mates bunched up. The tongue coasted ahead and drew the teams into a knot.

With a startled curse the driver jerked upright. Instantly the messenger leveled his gun, nervously on the watch.

"Tree down," spat the driver.

"Ain't been no wind," said the messenger in a high-pitched voice.

The driver looped the reins and stood up. Yellow light splashed on the bright ax.

"Road agents!" yelped the driver, diving for his Henry.

The two stood there shivering in the chill night, staring around the stage at the tall, whispering pines. Minutes passed.

Nothing happened.

"Some damned fool was just getting firewood or something," said the driver.

"We better wait," cautioned the messenger. "You know why."

The driver waited.

And still nothing happened.

"If this is a robbery," said the driver, "it's the funniest I ever saw. Hell with it. There ain't nobody here. Come on down and help me chop that damned tree out of the road."

"I got to stay here," said the messenger, glancing at the express box beside his boot. "You know why."

"You're lazy, that's all," snapped the driver peevishly. He climbed down, taking a lantern with him, and walked forward to straighten out his team and back them up.

That done, the driver turned his attention to the log. It was not a very big tree, about ten inches in diameter. Muttering to himself, he pried up the ax and fell to work.

Chips flew like pigeons into the outer darkness. One end of the log dropped down. The driver attacked the other with vigor. Presently, with a groan, that end splintered off and into the road.

The wiry driver then tried to lift the log by himself, but it was too heavy for his small strength.

"Damn you, Bob," he railed. "You come down here and quit that looking like a setter on a point. There ain't nothing going to happen."

"I got to stay here," complained the messenger.

"The sooner we get going the better, and we won't get going if I can't move this log." The driver stamped his boot and swore. "I need help!"

The messenger stayed tenaciously to his post. The driver argued and threatened. His temperature rose up to the cracking point. The horses stamped nervously, not very sure who was being bawled out.

Finally the coach creaked mysteriously as though of its own volition. The door hinges whined. With a grunt Jake Humphrey stepped into the light.

"I ain't supposed to do this," growled Jake, "but we got to get going sometime tonight." He stalked along the team to the driver, stooped and put his thick arms around the log and heaved with a grunt.

The coach creaked again, as mysteriously as before. The messenger was watching forward because that place had the most light on it.

A sure, steady hand wrapped itself around the messenger's rifle barrel.

"Easy now," said Chinook, his breath like ice water on the back of the messenger's neck.

"J-J-J-Jesus!" chattered the messenger as the rifle left his hands and soared outward and into the dark.

The resulting crash of the Henry's fall brought Jake and the driver up with a jerk.

"Easy," said Chinook, louder than before. "Shuck your guns, gentlemen."

Jake and the driver found themselves staring into the glare of the lamps. They could see nothing on the box but two vague shadows and they were not at all sure that one of them was the messenger.

Hurriedly, the driver shucked.

But Jake either had less sense or more guts. Jake snatched for his short gun. His hat sailed gracefully off his head. Jake changed his mind and dropped the short gun into the dirt.

"Turn around," said Chinook, through the curling powder smoke from his Peacemaker.

Jake and the driver turned with alacrity.

"I want you gentlemen to know," said Chinook, "that this isn't a holdup."

Jake barked a laugh. "It don't look like no Sunday-school picnic."

"I'm doing this in the name of the law. Here, look at this star, messenger."

"Anybody can tote a star," jeered Jake.

"I've been duly sworn and I've got a paper which entitles me to confiscate this express box."

36

The messenger was very amazed to behold such a thoroughly authorized road agent. He stared dumbly at the injunction Chinook held sideways at him.

"Okay," yelled Chinook.

A horse moved in the trees. Deke Murphy came out leading a pack animal. Deke climbed up and lowered the express box down to the crosstrees and threw a diamond hitch to hold it there.

After Murphy had led the loot away, Chinook carefully felt along the box for other weapons and found the driver's Henry which instantly followed the messenger's.

"I'm covered from the woods," said Chinook, "so don't try anything."

The three stood with their hands carefully held high. Chinook slipped down from the box and to the large boulder. He sprinted for Wild Cat, mounted and spurred down the road.

The last he saw of Jake and the driver, they were scrambling in the dirt trying to find their guns. The messenger was staring with open mouth and not doing a thing.

Chinook laughed into the crisp wind which cooled his face. He swung off into the timber, curved down a stream to meet Deke and, after an exchange of locating whistles, rode up to him.

They continued at a brisk trot, going deeper into the canyon along the stream to cover their tracks.

In a short while they reached an overhanging cliff which gave protection from both wind and sight.

Deke lighted a small, almost invisible fire. Chinook picked up a big boulder and began to splinter the express box.

"I still don't see how you can get away with it," said Deke. "I don't think there'll be enough money there to pay up half that loan. And Kendall will shore comb these hills for you now."

"We'll take that chance," said Chinook, smashing the box one last time.

The lid fell apart. The small fire glittered on metal.

Chinook swiftly knelt beside the splintered loot. His eyes grew cold and his hands were clenched.

"That dirty, double-crossing coyote!" stormed Chinook. "He's outguessed me! He knew that I'd stop that stage! He even planted a hidden gunman to snipe me off if I popped up. That filthy—"

"What's the matter?" said Deke.

"This ain't gold!" snapped Chinook. "We've gone and robbed that stage of a hundred pounds of lead!"

Chapter Six

THE chill gray fingers of dawn pointed from the eastern horizon. None too warm in his slicker, Chinook lay upon a flat red chunk of granite on the tip of a table butte, his telescope following the movements of a group of three riders.

He knew nothing of their identity save that they belonged, at the moment, at so much a month, to Kendall.

Riding abreast of each other but with a hundred yards or more as the intervals, they were thoroughly combing the prairie and coulees for any sign of Chinook Shannon.

Farther to the west another group went through similar movements. Kendall was sparing no effort to locate his game.

A rock moved behind Chinook and he whipped about, rolling into cover and snatching at his Peacemaker.

But it was only Deke.

"I had a hell of a time getting back from Bull Butte," complained Deke. "Kendall's even got his pumpmen scouring the country. I almost slammed straight into Steve and Lippy, but they didn't see me."

"You get any news?"

"Well," said Deke, "not so very much. I got hold of Sloppy Morris, the Diamond Palace barkeep. He's friendly, but he don't know very much." Deke sat down, produced some rocky biscuit and some jerked beef and laid them on a stone.

Chinook wolfed a sandwich, sloshed it down with a swig from his canteen and said, "Did you find out anything at all?"

Deke grinned and then laughed. "You know Taggart. Well, they run Taggart out of town last night right after you left. Maybe they didn't run him out. Maybe he just thought it would be smarter to leave. Anyhow, the last anybody seen of Taggart, he was scorching dirt bound north."

Chinook laughed with him, quite heartlessly. "He was bound to cut and run sometime. I guess I sort of gave him some momentum. You say Kendall is looking every place?"

"Yep. He's madder'n a gutshot grizzly about us sticking up that stage. Maybe he was peeved because you got away."

"That's funny," said Chinook. "I wonder just why he's so anxious to dry-gulch me. I don't know such a hell of a lot and I haven't got any case at all after noon today, that is, in just five and one-half hours. Old Man Time will take care of me for him. At one minute after twelve, the benefits of all suits, liens, stock and monies will pass forever from Shannon control into the hands of Borden. Kendall ought to let it ride."

"It's a cinch he's worried. From a bluff back there I counted four parties looking around and Kendall himself was in one of them."

"Wait a minute," said Chinook, jolted by the idea which exploded in his head. "Wait. Look here, Deke. Jesus Christ . . . I mean . . . For God's sake, Deke, where's my horse?"

"Where you left it. What's the matter with you? Where are you going?"

"I'm heading straight up to the Shoshone mine."

"What?" shouted Deke. "You damned fool, they'll shoot on sight! What in the name of common sense do you want at the mine?"

"Trail along," said Chinook, excitedly.

Chinook scrambled down the slope of the butte, entered the canyon where the rifled express box lay, and saddled Wild Cat. Deke, with loud and pessimistic protests, could do nothing but mount and swing down the stream bed after Chinook.

Keeping in ravines and dry coulees, Chinook worked his way around the north side of Bull Butte several miles out from it, continued northwest and finally arrived at the upper end of the canyon which contained the Shoshone mine.

Either by luck or a skill bred of imminent danger, they had not encountered anyone on the way. But they had no time to cover their trail. It showed plainly on the soft sand of dry bars, at the base of clay banks and in the moist moss of occasional wooded stretches.

Chinook realized that his only hope of evading discovery lay in quick movement. He would not let Deke stay with him after they came close to the mine. That was asking too much of the bowlegged little man. Deke, with protests, agreed to circle the canyon, carefully blotting his own tracks, and meet Chinook downstream in a short while.

It was now half past eight and the sun was growing warmer

as it rose to an inexorable zenith. Chinook watched his shadow shorten with great apprehension. When there was no shadow at all, his time of action was over. And there would be no shadow in just exactly three and one-half hours.

As they parted, Deke complained, "Look here, Chinook. You still got plenty of time to pull out of this. We can hit for Powder River. I know a place where we can get a couple jobs . . ."

"Me and Wild Cat," said Chinook, "rode all the way from Arizony to tell my grandad . . . well . . . So long, Deke."

Riding carefully, Chinook approached the rim above the place he had first spotted a guard. In a way he had all the advantage with him. Kendall thought that the mine was the last place in the world to hunt for Chinook Shannon. Guards, workers and gunmen, intrigued by a flat offer of a five-thousand dollar bounty, had scattered out with great enthusiasm.

The guard was gone.

Chinook was very relieved. He did not like the idea of shooting loud and emphatically in enemy country, nor did he enjoy the thought of chopping a man in cold blood.

Leaving Wild Cat in an abandoned prospect hole which had been trenched on the steep slope, Chinook slipped down toward the shacks.

He stopped every few paces to listen and was finally rewarded by the sound of singing in the cook shack.

The song was Chinese and therefore, Chinook reasoned, so was the cook.

He rounded the corner of the bunkhouse and almost fell over a red-shirted gentleman who sat with a rifle across his baggy knees.

Chinook withdrew hurriedly. Nothing happened to break the jangle of the Chinese song. Chinook looked around the corner and saw that the guard, feeling peaceful and secure, was contentedly dozing.

Cat-footing closer, Chinook suddenly jammed his Peacemaker into the guard's short ribs, snatching simultaneously at the rifle.

The guard came up fighting, hands solidly gripping the stock, half-asleep but obeying instinctively the impulse of self-preservation.

Chinook raised his Peacemaker and put a dent in the man's hat crown. With a gurgle, the guard melted against him.

Chinook carried the unconscious man inside and gagged and bound him. Presently the man struggled again. Chinook left him.

Scouting the other shacks with great care, without in the least disturbing the culinary artistry of the Chinese in the cookhouse, Chinook located Kendall's office and slipped inside.

He closed the door and bolted it. Holstering his Peacemaker, he looked around the littered interior. The floor was spotted with tobacco juice; the rough desk was scarred with burning but forgotten butts. In the corner squatted a black, gold-trimmed safe, very battered, bearing the legend "Dreadnaught, Burglarproof Vault."

Chinook tampered restively with it. The legend meant

what it said. He dragged it bodily into the middle of the room, tipped it over on its back and tried to pry it open with a drill.

"Damn you," growled Chinook. "I got a legal right to gut you, but I'll be damned if you recognize law any more than your master."

He opened the office door and looked out. No one was in sight. His glance rested upon a small building, half buried in the ground, which flaunted a tattered red flag.

"Ah," said Chinook, with satisfaction.

He took the drill and walked rapidly to the small building's front. He made hash of the padlock and pried the door open. The acrid odor of dynamite hit him.

He picked up a case and lugged it back to the office. Another trip netted him fuse and caps.

He had seen it done, but he had never tried it. He knew that dynamite would shatter a metal plate if only laid on the top of it, and as this dynamite in the box was something like seventy-five percent nitroglycerin, its shattering qualities were extraordinary.

He took a copper cap and inserted the fuse into the end of it and tied it there with a string, not liking the idea of biting it together. He then tied three sticks together and laid them on the top of the safe door.

He scouted the shacks again and presently found a bucket which he filled with muck. This he used to cover his charge after he had laid the fuse in against the sticks.

He opened the door and lighted the fuse and backed

hurriedly outside. He rounded the corner of the bunkhouse and stopped.

The explosion shook the camp and rocked the canyon echoes. Greasy smoke spewed forth from the shattered windows of the office, but he could not wait, after that noise, for the fumes to clear.

The Chinese cook saw him enter the office again and, shrieking in three dialects, the little man rapidly went away from there.

Chinook pawed through the smoke to the safe. The word "Burglarproof" had been blown squarely in two, leaving a greatly deranged "Burglar" to stare accusingly up from the shattered face.

The safe contained no money. Chinook had known that it would not. Chinook scooped up vast quantities of papers and dumped them on the floor. Kneeling with the smoke choking him, he flipped through the documents.

With eager fingers he seized a mining patent and opened it. It was all very regular. It stated that George Stewart, having done a hundred dollars of improvement on this claim every year for five years, was hereby granted a patent upon it.

It was signed by a peculiar mark, a crudely drawn pot on a cross-stick fire. Puzzled, Chinook frowned thoughtfully. "Stewart . . . George Stewart . . . Stewart . . . All Stewarts known as . . . Well, for God's sake, his mark was a stewpot, short for Stew Stewart."

It was witnessed as a signature by Chinook's grandfather.

Chinook thrust it into his batwing pocket and searched

the pile again. At last he uncovered a legal-looking document written in graceful hand, dated some six months before, which seemed to be a sort of abstract and mentioned the patent.

It deeded the patent, it said, for a certain consideration to Paul Borden, Bull Butte Bank, and it was signed again with a stewpot. An added paper stated that the mine was hereby sold to Brad Kendall in consideration of a certain sum and one dollar silver. . . .

The hammer of hard-ridden horses thundered down the canyon.

Chinook leaped up, started for the door and saw Kendall at the head of half a dozen men riding straight up at the office, guns drawn.

Whirling, Chinook dived through the glassless rear window and hit running.

Forty-four slugs plowed ground close to his jangling jingle bobs. His checkered shirt tugged at his arm.

"Kill him!" shrieked Kendall. "Take your Henrys! Dismount! Kill him!"

The six-gun fire let up for an instant. Chinook dived over the ore dump, scrambled up the steep canyon wall and leaped into the prospect hole. Wild Cat shied at him. Chinook mounted without touching stirrups and raked hard.

Startled and aggrieved, Wild Cat went straight up and came down heading the other way. At a panic-quickened run, the horse spread himself, charging up the slope toward the rim.

A slug jolted into the cantle. Another screamed away from under Wild Cat's chest, missing with more than an inch to spare.

Chinook reached the rim and plunged along the crest, over and out of sight. Yells of anger exploded behind him, quickly blotted by the ring and clang of flying hoofs in swift pursuit.

Chinook cut down toward the end of the canyon. On his right, far away, he could see the small doll-house buildings of the Slash S. He could see the knoll back of the house and wondered fitfully if he would arrive there eventually feet first or on horseback straight up.

The flowing breeze cleared the powder fumes out of his lungs and stimulated him.

He looked back and saw that Kendall and his six had been joined by another three. Hot for blood, the cavalcade was stringing out, riding low, sending hopeful lead singing across the plains.

Chinook spotted Deke.

Deke swung out of a coulee on his running mount and swerved in beside Chinook.

"You got 'em on our necks!" yelled Deke into the roaring windstream. "You find anything?"

"Yep!"

"What?"

"Ride!"

They plunged down a bank, splashing through ruined, whitish Pan Creek and up the other side. They leveled out on the plain again.

"Where we going?" shouted Deke.

"Bull Butte!"

"Jesus!"

"Ride!"

In a geyser of dust they skidded down another coulee, turned and raced along the hard bottom, whisked around a curve between the banks and straightened out running.

"Prepare to shift horses!" yelled Chinook.

"Shift what?"

"Horses! This Wild Cat is easy recognized. Shift hats and shift horses. Nobody can catch you on Wild Cat!"

"What the hell . . . ?"

"Stop! Shift!"

Chinook flung himself off, pulled Deke down, jammed on Deke's hat and swung up on Deke's roan.

"Head north. Head anyplace!" ordered Chinook. "They can't catch you on Wild Cat. Keep going!"

"But you . . ."

"I'm heading for Bull Butte."

The thunder of the approaching ten grew loud in their ears. Keeping to the plain, Kendall hoped to intercept the pair when they came out of the twisting coulee.

Deke dug spur. Wild Cat loped up the bank toward the north, went over and leveled out, long legs eating space.

Chinook went straight ahead, turned into a clump of tall alders and drew rein.

Kendall's bellow rose above the pounding hoofs. "There he goes!"

"Where's Deke?" shouted another man.

"To hell with Deke!" roared Kendall. "Get that Shannon!"

The ten swept down the bank and up the other side, leaving a yellow haze of dust behind them. Their yells faded.

Chinook neck-reined Deke's roan into the coulee bottom and went at a canter, unwilling to raise too much dust. Presently he came to a bottleneck choked with alders.

He spurred up to the plain again.

Far north he could see the small dots which were the rapidly disappearing horsemen.

The cloud of their passage parted a little and showed one man sitting a motionless horse behind the running nine.

Chinook put his telescope on that lone rider.

Kendall had stopped.

Why?

Chinook headed toward Bull Butte again. From time to time he looked back, but he had gone a mile or more before he again saw Brad Kendall.

With quirt and spur, Kendall was racing toward Bull Butte, almost parallel to Chinook.

They saw each other at the same time.

Chinook's quirt popped on the roan's rump. The cayuse speeded up.

Kendall was keeping his interval, evidently more interested in getting to Bull Butte than he was in nailing the man he took to be Deke Murphy.

Chinook saw that Kendall would again have to cross the coulee, which would give the roan a considerable lead.

The blasting at the mine and this ride had taken time. Too much time.

The sun was spinning almost overhead and the flying shadow under the roan's belly was almost at its minimum.

Chinook Shannon's time as a beggared and beleaguered cattle king was drawing to a close.

If he failed and lived, he knew that he would never be able to visit the Slash S and that grave behind the house. If he failed and died, he had at least tried.

But he had no thought of failure now in the heat of excitement. He had to get to Bull Butte before Brad Kendall, and he had to take the chance that none of Kendall's gunmen would spot him on the street.

Chinook changed his course slightly. The battered buildings of Bull Butte were rising out of the prairie like so many square scabs, malignant upon the otherwise clean face of the world.

Kendall was out of sight, crossing the coulee.

Chinook applied the quirt and sped along not much higher than the tops of the waving brown buffalo grass.

Chapter Seven

A T Chinook's larruping approach, two dogs dived under the Diamond Palace porch, a cat yowled in terror and soared straight up the side of the sheriff's office.

Backed with rolling, blanketing dust, his lathered roan set all four feet and skidded to a stop outside the bank, reared and came down again.

The Diamond Palace doors crashed outward and Jake Humphrey's fat-meat face opened to emit, "Shannon! Everybody out!"

Jake's hand dug faster than it had ever dug before. The short gun spewed flame. The bullet passed the instant after Chinook left the saddle. Across leather, Chinook chopped down.

Jake spun around in a half circle, a bullet through his shoulder. Chinook dived into the bank and the frightened roan left hurriedly for a more peaceful country.

Borden stood halfway up at his desk and then his legs became paralyzed and he stood just like that with half-crooked knees.

Chinook presented a horrifying sight. Smoke drooled from the big Peacemaker's muzzle, psychic flame shot out of Chinook's angry eyes.

"You crook!" he shouted at Borden. "I . . ."

*The short gun spewed flame. The bullet passed the instant after
Chinook left the saddle. Across leather,
Chinook chopped down.*

Another horse was arriving. The cashier was grabbing for his desk gun. Chinook went past Borden like a wind devil, upsetting chairs and sending paper flying in every direction.

Borden thought his day of judgment had arrived. His knees finally caved.

But by that time Chinook was past the sprawling cashier and into the open door of the big, steel-lined vault.

Chinook whirled and watched the door.

Borden had disappeared on the outer side of his desk. Kendall flashed by outside, wheeled and threw himself off his horse and started for the bank door.

A faraway yelp from one of Kendall's men cried, "Shannon's in there! Look out!"

Kendall dodged and ducked out of sight.

Boots sounded on the boardwalk and then everything was still.

Everything except for the big pendulum clock Chinook could see from the vault.

It was ten minutes of twelve and with a carefree and heartless tick-tock, tick-tock, the swinging brass disc was pushing up the seconds and minutes at an alarming rate.

The vault door was about three feet by six and the vault itself was about eight feet by eight. As Chinook had noted at first glance, the place was a perfect fort unless somebody outside began to play billiards with bullets and carom them off the steel walls. No one could enter the front door or attempt to close the vault door without being seen from the vault, and there was so little light in the money-tomb that no one outside could see into it.

A window splashed bright glass slivers into the bank. Boots scraped on the wall, but Chinook could not see what had happened.

Kendall snarled, "Where is he?"

Borden quavered, "He's in the vault. W-Would you please get him out of there. I . . . I don't like to have him in there. He . . . he's disrupting business, Kendall."

"I'll disrupt *his* business," Kendall promised. "Get down." Boots scraped. A board creaked. "Shannon. Come out of there with your hands high or I'm coming in after you!"

"Come ahead," said Chinook, audibly cocking his Peacemaker.

A .44 barked thunderously. The slug hit the steel lining, changed course, hit the back wall, shot sideways and up, embedding itself in some sacks which stood upon a shelf. Black, sandy stuff trickled out and down Chinook's neck.

Another shot whipped wickedly through the place. Chinook's ears hurt with the sound of it.

He had to have more cover. Kendall could stand there and do that all day and at least one shot would take effect.

Chinook reached up and pulled at the leaking sack. It was very heavy.

Placing it on the floor and lifting down others, Chinook built himself a barricade about three feet high and lay down behind it.

Kendall steadily combed the walls with ricocheting slugs. Finally he stopped and listened. "I guess that got him."

Chinook waited hopefully. But Kendall evidently was not sure.

The clock on the wall said eight minutes to twelve.

A rifle barrel appeared across the street, jutting out of a window. Chinook caught a glimpse of it and raised up. The gunman was trying a carom at the ceiling which would be extremely fatal.

Chinook had to fire. He slammed a slug through the bank glass. The rifle hastily withdrew.

Kendall growled, "You come out or we'll burn you out."

"Burn?" choked Borden. "B-But my bank . . . !"

"I'll pay you for your loss. It won't be much, and it's worth plenty dollars to me. . . ."

"No!" shrieked Borden from behind his desk. "No! No!"

"What the hell's the matter with you?" snapped Kendall.

"There's plenty the matter with him," said Chinook from the vault.

"Kill him, Kendall," begged Borden. "He's a mad dog. He'll shoot all of us. He's crazy!"

"Like a fox," said Chinook. "You know what's in here, Kendall?"

"I'll find out after we carry you away feet first," promised Kendall, slamming another bullet at random into the vault.

The spurting black stuff in the bags stung Chinook's eyes. He rubbed them clear and spat to rid his mouth of the gritty substance.

"Kendall," said Chinook, "I even hate to see a killer and a crook make a jackass out of himself."

"Isn't there some way to get him?" whined Borden hopelessly.

"Sure," said Chinook. "I can be got. Just walk right in here and see for yourself."

Kendall had stopped to load. He started shooting again.

Chinook reached up between shots and raked out file drawers, letting them scatter on the floor.

"What are you doing in there?" shouted Borden.

"I'm a bank examiner," said Chinook, "and I'm busy examining a bank."

"Kill him, Kendall," begged Borden.

"Ah," said Chinook, delighted at a find. "I've reached K and here I find Kendall. Kendall, Brad, Shoshone Mining Company. 'Dear Mr. Kendall: I have a very rich mine here in Bull Butte which, after your disappointments in the Bitter Root, should improve your fortunes. . . .'"

"Kill him!" shrieked Borden.

"You hadn't ought to keep copies of your letters," reproved Chinook, rattling paper.

Kendall stopped shooting. The clock on the wall said six minutes to twelve.

Chinook chortled, "And listen to this! 'Received March third of Paul Borden, Bull Butte, Montana, two thousand five hundred head of prime beef at fifteen dollars a head. . . .'"

"Ooooh," moaned Borden.

"So that was it," said Chinook. "You rustled Slash S stock after my grandfather was killed. Four thousand head there were. Maybe fifteen hundred died from that Pan Creek cyaniding and you sold the other twenty-five hundred and nobody ever thought to count the dead stock. My, my, my, Borden, you certainly keep your records in fine shape."

"What the hell are you into, Shannon?" demanded Kendall.

"Papers," said Chinook. "Come on in and look them over. I won't shoot you unless I get a good look at you."

"You won't shoot nobody," snapped Kendall. "Hey, Lippy! Get outside the window where he can't see and bounce a few off his ceiling."

"You bet," said Lippy, outside.

"Well, well, well," crowed Chinook. "Look here. My grandfather had three thousand in a checking account and it's still there."

"It's been subtracted from the loan!" wailed Borden, squirming so much that he moved the desk a little.

Chinook laid aside the file, reloaded his Peacemaker and ducked a slug from the street. With quick down-throws, Chinook blasted the whole bank window out. Glass spattered. Lippy, badly cut, yelled and retreated.

It was three minutes of twelve.

Chinook pulled out more files. In spite of everything he had found, he had not bettered his position in the least. Kendall evidently knew all about the whole transaction.

"Funny," said Chinook.

"What's funny?" said the invisible Kendall.

"The way you foxed me on that gold shipment," replied Chinook.

"The way I what?" yelped Kendall.

Chinook grinned wickedly to himself and patted his barricade. "You were shipping concentrate, weren't you, Kendall?"

"You ought to know!"

"I do," said Chinook. "But somehow, Kendall, I can't find any receipts from the government in here."

"I don't care what you can't find," retorted Kendall.

"Please, Mr. Kendall," whimpered Borden. "Kill him quick."

"No government receipts in here," said Chinook. "Not a one. Just a whole lot of concentrate. Maybe two hundred thousand dollars' worth."

"What?" snapped Kendall in amazement.

"I said, there's no use shooting in here at me. I'm laying behind two hundred thousand dollars' worth of concentrate. At least that's what Borden's records show, and it sure looks like it too. Good solid stuff. I'm glad Borden kept it."

"Borden . . . Borden kept it?" said Kendall, hoarsely.

"Sure," said Chinook, to his invisible audience. "You gave him concentrate to keep in his vault for shipment on the stage. He shipped lead bars to a friend in some other bank farther north. Borden paid your men for you, advanced you all the money you needed, gave you receipts for the gold and deposited the amount to your account. Then Borden was all set to get you killed just like he got my grandfather killed, snake out with all this gold and—"

"Borden," said Kendall in a hard, killer-cold voice. "Is Shannon telling the truth?"

"I swear to God, he's lying!" shouted Borden from under the desk.

"Not only that," said Chinook, "but Borden never owned the Stewart claim. Not a square foot of it. He had that patent here for safekeeping and when he persuaded you to kill off my grandfather, Borden forged a second agreement with a stewpot signature, overlooked a witness for it, which it has to have to be legal, and unloaded it on you. Soon as Borden foreclosed on the Slash S, the claim reverted to him, and even if he did sell it ahead of time, when his plans about killing you, Kendall, materialized, he had a legal right to all that range, the mine, this money which was to be held in escrow and later given to the Slash S in damages—"

A short, hard explosion jarred the bank. A Derringer leveled above the desk for a second shot.

Kendall grunted. Boots hit the boards hard. Kendall, clutching at his stomach, fighting to stay upright, staggered into view.

Borden bobbed into sight, smoke curling out of his Derringer's first barrel.

"Damn you, Borden," whispered Kendall, in agony. "Damn you . . . You've double-crossed your last . . ."

Borden was a sick green color. Kendall tried to level his .44. Borden was shaking.

Chinook yelled and dived forward to stop them.

Borden turned slightly, attention momentarily diverted. Kendall, dying on his feet, blood bubbling out through the fingers of his left hand, got the .44's terrific weight into position. His eyes were glazed with concentration. Borden turned and tried to shoot.

The .44 roared. The recoil flipped it out of Kendall's suddenly nerveless hand.

Borden's face was a smashed blot. He dropped across the desk.

Abruptly guns racketed out in the street. Chinook strode forward to the shattered window.

The sound increased in volume. Hoofs clattered. Men yelled.

With dust rolling behind them, the late Brad Kendall's riders fled the length of the town. Jake, Lippy and Steve grabbed mounts from the hitch rack and swung up and away.

"Kendall's dead!" yelled Jake.

They were gone.

From the upper end of the street came hoofbeats again. A compact group of horsemen came to a halt in front of the bank.

Deke and Taggart were riding on either side of a solemn-faced, frock-coated gentleman.

Chinook knew none of the others, but the party had come armed for war. Chinook stepped outside.

"Shannon!" cried Deke. "Where's Kendall?"

"Dead."

"Where's Borden?"

"The guy at the bottom of this?" said Chinook. "Dead."

"At the bottom of it?" said the frock-coated man. "But see here, when Taggart routed me out this morning up at Bannock, he said that Kendall—"

"Chinook must have the goods," said Deke. "He wouldn't lie to you, Judge."

"Judge?" said Chinook.

"Judge Olsen and a few friends," said the frock-coated man. "You are Chinook Shannon?"

"I am."

"And you have everything cleared up and under control?"

"Everything in order," said Chinook, holstering his Peacemaker with a final-looking thrust.

"Well, as a matter of form, we'll convene a court. I haven't had a session here for some time, Shannon. Waiting for you, but it looks like you beat me to it. I . . . uh . . . rather disliked the idea of taking the initiative where a Shannon was concerned. Gentlemen, it appears that the shooting is over. After I sign a few death certificates and such, we'll adjourn to the bar."

"A splendid idea," said Taggart.

And a little later, when everything had been examined, and the concentrate signed over to the Slash S, and when the posse of prominent citizens had ferreted out the cashier from under the counter, and when receivers had been appointed for the Bull Butte Bank, the court adjourned to the Diamond Palace Saloon to drink to the health of Chinook Shannon, Cattle King.

Come and Get It

Chapter One

WHEN Bill Norton got off the train at Wolf Junction, he had not expected to be met, exactly, with a brass band. But because he was the new owner of the Bar N, he thought there'd at least be a rig in sight.

But the only things he could see, when the train rattled away to dwindle on the plains, were a station agent and a prairie dog. After some thought, Bill decided on the former.

"By the way," he began casually, "I was sort of expecting somebody to meet me here. I'm the new owner of the Bar N."

The grizzled old agent looked the stranger up and down in a casual, insulting way. He could not miss the screaming stamp of Easterner upon that narrow-brimmed hat, the well-tailored suit and the polished oxfords. True, Bill Norton was not bad to look upon, being broad of shoulder, handsome and young. But there wasn't enough windburn to the stranger's face for the station agent.

"Huh," said the agent, shifting his cud from right to left. "Bar N? That's what you think."

"I said," began Bill anew.

"I heerd ye," said the agent. "You think maybe I'm deef?" Thereupon he left Norton's trunk where it lay and stalked off into his office, where the telegraph was clicking.

For a while Bill hopefully waited for the old man to come

back but hope waned. At last, Bill reached down, up-ended his trunk, and with a boost tossed it up on his shoulder. It was a peculiar trunk, having broad bands of color around it so that they crossed on top.

Dust in the street of Wolf Junction was deep enough to seep into the top of the oxfords. The sun was molten brass, intent on soaking the last drop of moisture from the cracked boards of the weary shacks and false-fronts.

Wolf Junction, Wyoming was not particularly sparkling in the eyes of young Bill Norton. He dumped the trunk on the steps of the Golden Jubilee Hotel, Saloon, Restaurant, Billiard Parlor and Girls Girls Girls, and looked the town over. Bill sighed. Evidently there wasn't a soul awake at this early hour of eleven o'clock, though a broken lantern and some empty cartridges in the street attested a lively evening just passed.

Bill wandered inside. A bartender was mechanically polishing glasses as though such action would mysteriously conjure up drinkers.

"Beg pardon," said Bill cautiously. "But I just got off the train. . . ."

The bartender had taken in the hat, the Eastern suit. "Well, git back on agin. I ain't stoppin' you."

Bill cleared his throat nervously. "I thought maybe somebody would be in here to meet me. My name is Norton and I'm the new owner of the Bar N. I thought . . ."

But the bartender drowned out whatever Bill Norton thought in a gust of laughter and then went on polishing glasses.

"That's the truth," said Bill uneasily. "Dan Norton was my father."

The bartender came back and looked carefully into Bill's face, and then shook his head. "Hey, Dude! C'mere!"

Dude came out from a partitioned office and walked up, obviously the owner of this place.

"Say, look," said the bartender, "this gent says he's Dan Norton's boy."

Dude's lazy, insolent black eyes strayed up and down Bill. "Huh," said Dude. And then he eased his collar and chuckled, going back toward his office.

"Please," said Bill. "I thought somebody from the Bar N would be in here to meet me. I wired. They knew I was coming."

"Maybe they knew you too," said Dude, vanishing.

Bill looked disconsolately at himself in the glass. Personally he couldn't see anything wrong. Indeed there was nothing wrong except his clothes and complexion.

"How come?" said the bartender.

"How come what?" said Bill.

"You don't look like Dan Norton's boy ought to look," complained the bartender. "Y'ain't never been West before?"

"No. You see, my father left my mother in the East. I was going to come out after another year or two but my father's death made it necessary for me to leave right away. To get his affairs in order, of course."

The bartender laughed appreciatively.

"What's wrong with that?" challenged Bill.

"Sonny, I'm pretty shore you'll find everything in order.

Red Mike Doherty was appointed ex . . . exec . . . trustee by the bank." And the bartender found another occasion to laugh.

Bill's nerves couldn't stand much more. He went outside and hefted his trunk to his shoulder, and went on up the street to the livery stable. A mossy-bearded oldster dozed there, chair against the door, soaking up sunlight. He opened one eye lazily and looked at Bill. He closed his eye and then, as though just registering what he had seen, came swiftly erect.

"Huh," said the oldster. "Easterner."

"Yes, I beg your pardon but . . ."

"Don't beg mine," said the oldster, "it wasn't my fault you bought them clothes."

"I'm the new owner of the Bar N," said Bill. "I want to rent a horse so I can ride out . . ."

"Nope."

"Why not?"

"We ain't got no gentle hosses and we values them as we has got."

Bill sighed deeply and dropped his trunk. He took out a five-dollar bill and shoved it under the oldster's nose. "Now do I get a horse?"

"Reckon so," yawned the stable guardian, getting up and stretching. "But don't blame me if he throws yuh. And if he does don't go askin' for your five dollars back. A deal is a deal."

Norton sighed again, watching the old man saddle up a roan. And Bill Norton sighed once more, recognizing the inevitable. The roan was as swaybacked as a Flying U brand, as listless as a hound dog and as bowlegged as the hostler himself.

"I'll return him in a couple days," said Bill.

"Return him hell," replied the hostler. "Mister, you bought yourself a hoss and I throwed in the saddle and bridle."

Bill mounted and put his trunk on the horn. The roan, Beaney, shuffled forward.

Chapter Two

IT was sunset when Beaney finally slouched into the ranch house yard of the Bar N. Bill Norton had found the way only by grace of God and a certain sixth sense of his own. Certainly the men he had met had not been particularly explicit as to the route. But now he was here and at last, certainly, he would have an end to all the galling stares and "huhs!" which met his Eastern garb and Eastern pallor.

The place was apparently deserted, most of the men being gone on spring roundup, and so even here was a rousing welcome denied. A lamp was being lighted in a corner room and so Bill slid off and deposited his trunk on the ground to make his way toward this beacon.

He knocked and a rough growl answered, "Come in, what the hell are you waitin' for?"

Bill stepped inside. This room was the ranch office and its walls were heavy with racked rifles. The roll-top desk was colorless with its dust and strewn paper. Scattered about a spittoon on the floor were half a thousand or so cigar butts.

The man at the desk evidently hadn't expected Bill. Red Mike Doherty's eyes shot wide and then narrowed until they vanished beneath his shaggy brows.

"And who the hell are you?" said Red Mike, leaning back and hooking his thumbs into his cartridge belt.

"Bill Norton. I suppose you are Red Mike Doherty. I . . ."

"What did you come out here for?"

"Why," said Bill, startled, "after I was informed that my father was dead I . . ."

"What's that got to do with it?" challenged Red Mike in a voice so loud that for an instant Bill thought all the rifles had fired at once.

"Why . . . why, I'm his heir."

Red Mike laughed and beside that sound a rattler's buzz sounded congenial. "So you're his heir," chuckled Red Mike, looking at the Eastern clothes, taking in the absence of gun and sunburn. "Sonny, all the advice I can give you is to hop a train back to the land of pink tea. Yore old man's estate consisted of a secondhand brace of six-guns—them as is hangin' on that antler there. Take 'em and welcome."

Red Mike turned back to his tally sheets, dismissing Bill Norton from his mind.

Bill took down the worn six-guns and held them reverently. He unwound the belts from around the holsters and carefully took out one of the Colts. It had seen plenty of service, but it was polished and oiled and apparently in excellent shape. Bill pulled back the hammer and found it very heavy.

Suddenly an explosion shook the room. Red Mike's hat slapped violently against the far wall and the ricocheting slug went yowling out through the window, taking a pane of glass with it.

Red Mike leaped up, purple with wrath. "What the hell are you doin'? Jesus, if you don't know nothin' about guns, leave 'em for men to handle!" Wrathfully he advanced upon Bill and Bill, looking very apologetic, backed out of the door.

Red Mike pointed north. "Go grab a rattler and get the hell out of here before somebody makes buzzard bait out of you!"

Bill looked nervous. "I . . . I can't very well do that. You see . . . you see, I haven't got any money left. I bought a horse and . . ." He was shocked at the changeable moods of this Red Mike Doherty. The man had taken one look at Beaney and was now roaring with laughter.

"They been tryin' to sell that horse for a year to my knowledge. Sonny, did you lose yore nurse along the way?"

"I can't leave the place," said Bill, reverting to the subject with haste. "He won't carry me much further and I haven't had anything to eat all day."

Red Mike jerked his thumb toward the cook shack. "You maybe can find some cold beans in there if you look and there's some blankets in the bunkhouse. Tomorrow morning when this crowbait can walk, you hightail it back to Wolf Junction and clear out."

"But I told you I couldn't buy a railroad ticket," said Bill. He looked forlornly at Red Mike. "Couldn't you . . . maybe give me a job here?"

"A job? You?" cried Red Mike in glee. "And what the hell do you think you could do around a ranch?"

"Why . . . nothing, I guess. But you can't let me starve like this. Surely there's some kind of a job. I could tally . . ."

"What do you know about tallyin'?"

"I . . . I read about it in a book. If . . ."

"Huh!" said Red Mike, tired of laughing by now. "Sonny, I ain't made of iron. I got a heart. They need a second-string belly robber . . ."

"A what?"

"A second cook at Camp Three. You can take it in the morning. If you don't know how to peel spuds now, Greasy Gates 'll learn yuh."

Bill, dazed as one who has fallen a great distance, stumbled back to his horse and sorrowfully led the animal through the dusk toward the corrals.

"Get your trunk," said Red Mike, pushing it over with his boot. "Huh, leave it to a damned dude to pretty up his warbox. Yellah and green and orange stripes! Ain't there never no end to yore damn foolishness?"

Bill shouldered the trunk and trudged away.

Red Mike watched him go with narrow eyes and then shrugged to turn back to his office and the tally sheets.

Bill put the trunk in the bunkhouse and then gave the woeful Beaney a can of oats and a rubdown. It was a very new thing in the life of Beaney and he showed a mild interest in the proceedings, glancing back now and then at the Easterner's activities.

Giving the horse a consoling pat on the shoulder, Bill started toward the cook shack. The ranch was as quiet as death and it weighed heavily upon his spirits. He struck a light to a lantern and looked into a pot which sat upon a greasy table. Bill made a face. Those beans had been sitting there for a week at least, and the dried brown sludge was almost more than his stomach could stand. However, he was hungry and he stirred up the mess, added some water, and then got some sticks and lighted the fire to warm his supper. He put two hardtack biscuits in the oven to preserve his teeth and at last he dined.

It was a very thoughtful meal with long pauses in between mouthfuls. But it was also a fruitful meal since he had an idea by the time he had finished it. He went for a walk around the buildings, stumbling over the unfamiliar ground since he did not carry the lantern.

After considerable search he found the ranch cemetery. It was fenced in on a bare knoll and not one blade of grass was there to soften the hard cracked earth. Cautiously he struck a match or two and looked at the rough boards with which some of the graves were marked. The rain had lightened the whitewash until through it could be read "Best Dried Apples" and "Crunch-Crunch Crackers." Lumber was scarce on these prairies. Too scarce to be wasted on dead men.

At last he located his father's grave. He stood beside it for some time, lost in the gloom of the evening. Finally he shook off the dark mood and trudged back to the buildings to search for a shovel.

For the next hour he carefully dug into the flinty soil, not knowing how deep the body would be. But men had had other things to do the day they had buried Dan Norton and the grave was shallow.

It was not a pleasant task and the original state of the beans did not help. But despite all that, Bill persevered, uncovering the whole of the corpse with his hands and then, kneeling in the grave, made a careful examination. He had used up four matches when he at last found a bullet wound. It was in the back of the head. There was another between the shoulder blades and a third in the arm. Bill raised the arm slowly until it extended above the head. Not until then did his finger slide into the wound.

It took considerable courage with his sensitive stomach to put the body back in order again. But when he had finished there was little to show that the corpse had been disinterred.

Bill walked slowly back to the bunkhouse. He dropped the shovel in the corner and then lighted the lamp on the table. By its light he reread the telegram he had received from the banker of Wolf Junction, Brad McNeil.

WILLIAM NORTON
21 E. 8TH ST.
NEW YORK CITY

YOUR FATHER KILLED IN ACCIDENT BY WILD HORSE. BRAD McNEIL

Bill put the telegram away and rolled into the lowest bunk, to lie staring for hours out through the doorway at the bright Western stars.

Chapter Three

THE crew at Camp Three was incredulous and with one glimpse of Beaney and rider, all dawn grouches were gone. But outside of a few stifled snorts no real noise was made, since men didn't laugh around Red Mike Doherty lest he suddenly get it into his head that he was the target—which he never could be.

Red Mike pulled up before the chuck wagon where Greasy Gates was slamming breakfast together with an air which indicated that every chunk of sowbelly had personally insulted him an instant before. He got that way whenever he had to peel his own spuds.

"Greasy," said Red Mike, "here's something for you to make into a helper."

Gates looked up almost with joy and then scowled. But nobody ever found any fault with Red Mike's ideas. Nobody. Not ever. Bill got down and pulled the battered saddle off Beaney and sent the aged horse out toward the remuda with a slap. Dropping the saddle, Bill took off his coat and laid it aside. Rolling up his sleeves, he approached the fire.

Everybody was silent until Red Mike rode out toward the herd and then, appreciatively, the crew gathered round.

Greasy looked Bill up and down with disgust. Bill, in his

turn, examined the cook. Greasy Gates had a cleaver in one hand, an unlighted cigar in his mouth and a derby hat on the side of his bullet head. About him was girded a flour sack black with abuse.

"I hear tell," said Greasy, "that Red Mike left a helper around here. But I don't see nothin'. Do you, boys?"

Carefully the crew looked all around, even under the wagon, and then came back shaking their heads. "Nothin' at all, Greasy."

Bill turned red and said nothing. But he did see that the breakfast was starting to go up in smoke and he made a move to pull the frying pan off the fire.

With one hard kick, Greasy sent the pan soaring and almost broke Bill's wrist. "If I sees somethin' that needs to be done, I'm the gent that's goin' to do the sayin' that it's got to be done. Have you got that straight, Pretty Boy?"

Bill nursed his wrist.

"Now go get that pan and put it back where you found it," said Greasy.

Bill didn't move. Greasy, cleaver gripped resolutely and cigar working in his mouth, advanced to tower over Bill. "You hard at hearin', Pretty Boy?"

Bill said nothing. He retrieved the pan. And just as suddenly the punchers lost interest in him. They got their pans and got their breakfast and somehow Bill got through his first half-hour of being a second cook.

When breakfast was done, the punchers threw their pans into a pile beside the fire, eyeing the newcomer covertly to see what he would do. And Bill picked up the pans and stacked them neatly, looking around for a bucket in which to carry water up from a spring below the wagon. And again the punchers lost interest to go their several ways.

Greasy Gates, when they were alone in camp, sat down on a rock and crossed his arms in front of him, cleaver in full view. "As soon as you git them dishes washed, start in on the pans. And as soon as you got them pans shinin'—and I mean shinin'—you can start in peelin' spuds. And as soon as you get them peeled, you can get some chips for the fire. And as soon as you get them, you can fill up the drinkin' barrel. And then we'll get to work."

Bill looked sideways at Greasy Gates now and then as he worked but the cook was a colossus among cooks, and though Bill hadn't been short-changed on height, the difference was too great. Besides, he had to keep this job.

When the punchers rolled into the sougans that night, to heave a boot or two at Bill because he made so much noise washing the supper dishes, Bill was ready to quit.

His arms ached. His hands, unaccustomed to such things, were red and raw. His heels felt as though they had been driven up into the back of his neck. When he finally crawled into bed, he put out one hand to touch the holstered guns, but the contact had not been made for an instant when Bill was sound asleep.

But not for long—or so it seemed to him. Two hours before the sun was up, Bill was busy building the breakfast fire. He found out that two breakfasts had to be served. One to the riders going out and one to the night riders coming in. And so he toiled in the ink which overspread the plains and wondered how long he could keep it up without dropping in his tracks.

But he did keep it up. Greasy Gates saw to that. With threat and curse, Greasy Gates ran the show from the shade of the chuck wagon, only deigning to put the meals themselves together.

Throughout a hot day, Bill sweated outwardly and boiled inwardly. And again when night came, he died. But Greasy Gates resurrected him with a kick and life went on.

For five long days Bill hung between life and death. He was too weary to think. His hands mechanically did Greasy Gates' bidding and that was the end of it.

But even such work has its compensations. On the sixth day he found that he could speed up a little, enough to get ten seconds rest. And on the seventh he found that he was growing expert enough to get fifteen minutes rest. And by the time ten toilsome days had sped, he had a whole hour to himself every afternoon.

And as the days progressed he found a friend. Somewhere in his wanderings, Greasy Gates had come by a black-and-tan pup and because he saw the possibilities of not having to clean up the ground around the fire after gaining such a possession, he kept the dog with him.

But Tango did not lead a very happy life; the air about him was always too eternally full of frying pans and boots and blue scorchers. Tango meant well, but at night he answered the coyotes and by day, because the leftover food was not any too plentiful, he sometimes contrived the theft of a slab of sowbelly. His hunger must have been considerable at these times as he was invariably caught and kicked—and whatever else one might say about Greasy Gates, he certainly could kick.

A mysterious thing had begun to happen shortly after Bill's advent upon the Bar N. Tango's flanks filled out. Nobody remarked it but Tango's own temper had begun to smooth down. Heretofore the beatings had driven him into a very antisocial state of mind, but now he never so much as offered to show his teeth except—and here was the key—except when somebody came too close to Bill's sougan or strove to sit down on Bill's gaily colored trunk.

The rescued hour from the day went to Tango. And because nobody had ever thought the pup had brains except Bill, Tango prospered. Bill avoided such obvious things as asking for food and such indignities as sitting up. The training went into a very strange byroad. Out in the brush, in his hour of rest, Bill practiced a draw. And Tango practiced too. Tango, on command, would leap for the wrist drawing the gun. Further, Tango would leap on a back at Bill's order. Further, any specified object such as a coat or a hat or a boot would be fetched by Tango with a slyness rivaled only by a Mexican bandit.

The men had grown used to Bill's smudged presence. He no longer offered any interest, and besides, the work had to go on apace in this out-of-season roundup.

All in all it appeared that Bill Norton was going to sit by in perfect contentment and let everything of violence go by the boards. He practiced the draw, yes. But he had never fired but that one shot from his father's guns. And while a fast draw is pretty, any gunman will say that the draw without shooting accuracy is next to wasted energy.

Chapter Four

ONE afternoon the camp received a visitor due to the fact that Red Mike was making Camp Three his headquarters for the moment. Bill had his arms up to the elbow in a stack of greasy pans and was working furiously to retrieve a little more time for Tango's lessons and his own relief. But when he saw the stranger, Bill slowed up.

The man had the unmistakable stamp of a banker upon him. His broadcloth frock coat reached down to the top of his boots; a chain with a wolf's tooth in the middle stretched across his ample and embroidered vest; a bulge under the shoulder showed the position of a short gun. The man's face was puffy with easy living and his voice was husky with too many expensive cigars. This, without doubt, was Brad McNeil.

Red Mike rode in as the banker rode up. "Howdy, Brad."

"How is it coming, Doherty?"

"Well as can be expected. Lot of stock missing though, according to these tally sheets."

Brad McNeil climbed cumbrously down and seated himself on a saddle. The day was warm and he was perspiring amply. He mopped his brow and fanned his coat back and forth. Finally he yielded to an impulse and removed the dark garment, laying it behind him on a box of dried apples. It jingled when he did that. He loosened up his vest.

"So some stock is missing, huh? Maybe old Norton was too damned optimistic when he came to me for money."

"Yeah," said Red Mike, squatting on his heels and nursing the chill of a cup of water between his palms. "Looks that way."

"When will you be finished?" said Brad McNeil.

"Tomorrow afternoon should do the trick."

"Good."

As they talked, Bill was all ears. Finally he made a motion to Tango who lay sprawled under the chuck wagon. Tango came up with wagging tail and Bill bent toward his ear for an instant. Tango sobered immediately. Very slyly, after the habit of one versed in the art of thieving sowbelly, Tango crept up in back of McNeil, taking the coat in his teeth and quietly towing it back to Bill. It took Bill but an instant to retrieve the jingling keys and then he made another motion to Tango. The dog dragged the coat back and left it beside the apple box.

Bill grinned a little to himself. He had originally intended to use that trick for a few practical jokes, but fate had its own design.

McNeil and Doherty went on talking, all unawares. And at last, as McNeil got up to go, Bill stood back from the pans.

"You're Mr. McNeil, aren't you?" said Bill.

"Who's this?" demanded the banker of Red Mike.

"Old man Norton's boy," said Doherty.

McNeil was jolted. "What's he doing here?"

"Aw, I get softhearted once in a while," said Red Mike. "When he found out he didn't have any rights to the Bar N, he couldn't go back so I gave him this job so he could eat."

McNeil scowled.

"Someday," said Bill innocently, "I would like to check over the records, Mr. McNeil. That is, if you don't mind."

"Certainly, my boy. Certainly. I hardly expected you to come West. You were in a college someplace, weren't you?"

"Yes," said Bill.

"I heard Norton say so. Too bad about the old man, son."

"Wasn't it," said Bill innocently.

McNeil was only slightly annoyed to find that his coat had fallen off the apple box. He tossed it over his arm and then mounted.

"Be seeing you, Doherty."

"So long," said Red Mike.

The two went away from the chuck wagon in their different directions.

"What the hell are you doin'?" roared Greasy Gates, waking up in astonishment to see that Bill was idle.

Bill swiftly bent over the pans again and to their music Greasy Gates went softly back to sleep, dirty face pillowed on soiled arms. Tango, with the spirit of a pirate, stole his hat and dropped it in the ashes, turning back to Bill with wagging tail and lolling tongue. Bill grinned back but he was very much preoccupied.

Chapter Five

H E had not finished until all the camp was snoring. And strangely he was not tired this night. He stood by the remnants of the fire and stared out across the bluish plain to the ragged indigo hills above which glowed the tidings of the moon. Carefully, then, he trod over the sleeping figures and made his way to the sougan where slept Red Mike, shaggy head pillowed on his saddle, white sombrero lying to one side. He took the hat and pulled the neckerchief from inside it and then, wrapping stealthy fingers about a coiled riata, Bill slipped toward the rope corral where the top string mounts rested.

The big sorrel which Red Mike rode was close at hand and Bill did not have to try his luck with a throw. The sorrel reared once or twice, not liking to work at night, but finally Bill got the saddle in place and bit between the unwilling teeth. Silently he led the bronc away from the chuck wagon.

Tango came up, whimpering a little at this breach of routine.

"Go back," whispered Bill. "I'll be with you shortly."

Tango, not liking it at all, went back, looking at his departing friend over his shoulder.

As soon as Bill was outside the hearing radius from camp, the quirt popped and the startled sorrel lunged forward, breaking into a ragged gallop. Bill settled him down. It was a strange seat that he rode. Heels down and in, legs straight, back like a ramrod. The wind was hard and exhilarating against his lean face and the prairie sped beneath the spurning hoofs. Startled coyotes leaped aside from the trail, an owl whooshed skyward from its rabbit dinner. The ground rose and fell in sudden swoops but level and ravine were all alike to Bill and the quirt cracked again and again.

Finally faroff sparkled the lights of Wolf Junction. A train left a plume of sparks against a sable sky and the whistle came sweetened by the distance. Bill eyed the long series of yellow squares as they sped across the plain and wondered for a moment if it would not be better sense to climb aboard than to stay here and run the chance of getting a gut full of lead.

When he had reached the end of the single street, the train was gone and Wolf Junction had settled back to faro and redeye. Bill tied the sorrel behind a store and went forward on muted feet, well appreciating the target he made in that white sombrero. He came to the back of the bank and found a door.

His hands shook a little as he searched out the right key. It seemed to him as though he was beating upon an alarm gong instead of rattling keys. At last he found the one which fit and, with a glance about him, stepped gingerly into the bank.

A streak of moonlight spread itself like a gauze curtain over the file cabinets. Bill's fingers were swift as he rumpled the papers. But he found nothing under the name of Norton. He turned to the locked roll-top desk of the president. A key fitted at last and he opened the drawers to comb through the files there. Finally he found a paper which bore the name

Norton. Pocketing this, he went to the vault. It was old, built in the days when cattle had first come to Wyoming. And a combination lock was a stranger to it. The biggest key fitted here and the door loosed a dismal dirge as Bill swung it back. A lighted match showed him the filing case inside. And it was here that he found the important documents relating to the Bar N.

Slowly he closed the door and then, cat-footed, went back to the entrance. Suddenly a light was unmasked and its glare struck at him. But almost before that bull's-eye was focused, Bill drew and fired. With a crash and a shout of pain the darkness came back.

A bellowing voice roared, "Stand where you are!"

Bill answered with lead. The men behind the cages dropped hastily out of sight only to bob up an instant later to behold an empty doorway.

McNeil yanked his grazed watchman to his feet. "Get up, you fool! That was a helluva time to go to sleep!"

"What about you?" snarled the watchman.

"I said he'd get here as soon as I found my keys was missin'," snapped McNeil. "And I was right!"

"Ain't you goin' to follow him?"

McNeil moved ponderously to the door and stared into the moonlit plain. "There's only one way to find him in that. We'll head for Camp Three. Get Tom and some of the boys. We'll show that fool a thing or two!"

Chapter Six

IT was dawn and it looked just like any other dawn to Camp Three—which was all they knew about it. The fire was blazing and a stew was bubbling and the coffee was sending out its aroma in tantalizing veils and Greasy Gates sat up in his bunk in some astonishment at the fact that he had not been called.

Bill, strangely cheerful, banged violently upon a frying pan with a potato masher and yelled, "Come and get it before I throw it out!"

Night riders, hearing the summons slightly ahead of time, came galloping in. Tango, awaking to discover to his vast pleasure that Bill had come back after all, waltzed happily in toward the fire, wagging his greeting.

"Come on, you rannies!" shouted Bill. "Daylight's burning!"

The night riders dismounted, grinning at so much glee emanating from a usually obliterative second cook.

Greasy Gates rolled out of his sougan, not quite certain whether he was pleased or not. A stew for breakfast did not seem the usual thing and besides, there was something strange about that stew. Sowbelly and beans made up the diet but the aroma told a different story.

"What you got there?" said a night rider, sniffling pleasurably.

"I ran down . . . I mean I snared a couple jackrabbits last night," said Bill. "I thought maybe you'd like a change."

Several of the men were up and pulling on their boots. This was all very odd to them to see Greasy Gates still in bed and to smell that stew.

"Who the hell's cook around here?" roared Greasy Gates, grabbing the first thing which came to hand—a boot—and getting ready to lay about him.

"Lay off!" said the night rider. "I never seen you do nothin' for us but cook sowbelly."

Others agreed and Greasy Gates, promising himself satisfaction when the camp was deserted, made a show of calming down. Meantime plates were being piled up with the rabbit and potato stew. And it did Greasy Gates no good whatever to hear the men praise the quality of both stew and coffee.

"Guess he took your old socks out of the pot," said a rider to Greasy Gates.

Greasy Gates merely glared.

Red Mike came back from the rope corral. "Say, somethin's funny around here. Feathers is as wet as rain. He's been rode!"

Everybody was very busy eating and Red Mike sat down on a box and took his portion, staring before him in a puzzled way, occasionally turning to look back toward the rope corral.

Uneasily, Bill was busy handing out more stew and coffee.

A rider glanced up and then stared intently toward the north. "Somebody comin'."

"Hell of a lot of somebodies if you ask me," said Red Mike, standing up. "Wonder what the rush is all about."

Bill unobtrusively vanished around the end of the chuck wagon, pulling his father's guns from under the canvas cover and buckling them on.

Brad McNeil wasted no time. He expected a fight and when he didn't instantly get it he was astonished. He pulled in at the head of his half-dozen men and glared at Red Mike.

"What's the idea?" snarled McNeil.

Red Mike read fight in the tone. He hitched at his gun to make sure it was loose in its holster and then advanced a few paces. "I don't get you, McNeil."

"Sure, put on a bluff about it," snapped the banker. "I come for them papers you stole last night in Wolf Junction. Get 'em and get 'em fast. Keep 'em covered, boys."

Plates in hand, the Camp Three crew was in no position for war. Stupidly they stared at the leveled Winchester muzzles.

"I don't know what you're talkin' about," said Red Mike. "What papers?"

"You know damned well what papers," said McNeil. "I'm doin' business my own way without any interference from you. In case you ain't heard, bank robbin' is serious business. Don't think your horse wasn't seen and don't tell me I can't recognize you when I see you. Go on. Get those papers or somebody is going to get hurt."

Red Mike frowned. "Wait a minute, McNeil. If you're so damned sure I've got 'em you can search the camp. But damned if I can figure out what papers . . ."

"The Bar N papers, you fool!" roared McNeil. "Lefty, go through this place and don't quit until we've got what we want."

Red Mike watched the search begin. Sougans and flour

and bridles flew to the right and left while two men pawed over the dunnage.

"McNeil," said Red Mike, "maybe you tipped your hand. What is there about the Bar N that I don't know?"

McNeil scowled. "The mortgage papers," he countered swiftly. "I need 'em to foreclose and you know it. And as long as I can't foreclose you're in charge here. And what was that you said about cattle disappearin'?"

Red Mike's hard face froze. "I been called a lot of things—"

"Cover him," snapped McNeil.

"—but nobody ever had the guts before to call me rustler. Step down here and give me an even break or I'll pick you off the first time I meet you on the trail."

All the baggage except the violently painted trunk had been searched and now that came to light. Lefty pried off the lock and yanked up the lid. The Camp Three men, staring at Lefty's handiwork, grew somewhat round-eyed.

"Here's what you want, Brad," said Lefty, pulling forth the documents and extending them.

"Just keep holding them right there," said a soft voice on top of the chuck wagon.

All eyes jerked aloft to behold Bill behind two leveled Colts.

"Now hand those papers to Red Mike Doherty," said Bill. "He'll be interested to find out he was working for a crook."

"Get him!" shouted McNeil. "He can't shoot!"

A Winchester banged and, in the same explosion, the McNeil rider flung up his arms and lurched back into the dirt. McNeil wasted no time. He snatched at his short gun.

*All eyes jerked aloft to behold Bill
behind two leveled Colts.*

The Colts blazed. McNeil's hand was spattered red and the short gun leaped back and down.

Nobody there could believe such shooting from an Easterner. But prudence dictated that the McNeil riders drop their rifles slowly to earth.

"Take those papers, Doherty," said Bill.

Red Mike took them. He opened them up and, with squinted eyes, examined them. "Why," he said in some astonishment, "this is old Norton's will. I thought he didn't have none, McNeil. And look, here's a receipted deed to the Wolf Junction First National for the Bar N mountain pastures as payment in full for all loans and signed by McNeil. Hell, that's only a small chunk. Look here, McNeil, is this deed the straight goods?"

"Talk up," said Bill from on top of the wagon.

McNeil stared at the two motionless Colts and nodded dismally.

"Which means," said Red Mike, "that you didn't have no claim to foreclose on the Bar N. You stole these papers back after old Norton was shot from behind—*you shot Norton from behind!*"

"No!" yelled McNeil. "Lefty . . ."

Lefty leaped for the banker's throat but the night riders tripped him and held him down.

"Some of you boys," said Bill, "escort Mr. McNeil into Wolf Junction and give him to the sheriff. I'll be in to make the complaint this afternoon. And if the rest of you rannies have finished breakfast, you better be getting to work."

He climbed down off the chuck wagon to hit earth beside

Red Mike. McNeil was still staring in stupid disbelief at the Easterner.

Red Mike looked at the trunk and saw a pair of Wellington boots. "I thought you said you went to college in the East, Mr. Norton."

But Bill was already walking away. Greasy Gates did not realize that he was Bill's goal until it was too late. And then an earthquake rose up and hit Greasy Gates in the face. Bill picked the cook up again and gave him an expert wrestling heave to land him in a pile of pots. It was done so effortlessly that it seemed impossible that Greasy Gates could emerge from the ruin so bloody. Bill was advancing very coldly but Greasy Gates dropped to his knees.

"Please," moaned Greasy Gates, dazed and shaken.

"Get busy on those pots," said Bill, walking back to Red Mike. And Greasy Gates got busy.

The men were just gathering to take McNeil away, having been delayed by Bill's sideshow. But before he let himself be led from there, McNeil had a question.

"Mr. Norton," said McNeil in a faint voice, "I . . . I thought you said you went to a college."

"You said that," replied Bill. "And I did—of a sort." He started putting things back into his trunk. A saber, a pair of cavalry boots and a holstered single-action Army pistol. Then he closed down the lid, ornate with its regimental striping.

"The name of the place," said Bill with a quiet smile, "was West Point."

Story Preview

NOW that you've just ventured through some of the captivating tales in the Stories from the Golden Age collection by L. Ron Hubbard, turn the page and enjoy a preview of *Devil's Manhunt*. Join Tim Beckdolt, a man who strikes gold and is on the brink of a new life. When a killer jumps his claim and forces him to mine the remainder for him, Tim tries to flee. Soon he's being pursued in a bloodthirsty manhunt through vicious terrain.

Devil's Manhunt

AT fourteen, Tim had gone wandering across the West as a boy of all work, under the most indifferent masters, a runaway from a home that wouldn't have him. He had learned prospecting in two heartbreaking years under the absolute tyranny of old Scotty O'Rourke—who had outlived three partners and had tried to outlive Tim. The world-weary youngster now saw himself as a successful young man; he wanted a ranch of his own, fine horses to ride, and the wherewithal to influence the unkind.

At twenty-three he had it all within his grasp. Now and then he would straighten up, limber his back and gaze ahead of him. But he was not seeing red rocks and pines; he was seeing ranch houses, thousands of cattle grazing, white horse fences and himself in fine clothes. It was an innocent dream.

At four o'clock on the afternoon of July 13, it was shattered entirely and utterly.

A shadow fell across his sluice and Tim stopped, not looking back, but staring at the reflection in the cold blue gleam of a Winchester barrel.

The first words he heard bit deep. They were indifferently, even wearily, spoken. "Wait a minute, Sven, don't kill him."

Tim held on to the sluice box to keep his hands from

shaking. He turned carefully until he stood leaning against the rough, hard slabs, water curling around his ankles, sweat growing cold on his face. The man called Sven was rendered even more huge by his standing on the bank two feet higher than the water.

He was shaggy, with matted hair; his clothes were nondescript and slovenly. His face was big, with small eyes.

The other man was seated on a rock. He was young, handsome, about twenty-eight and dressed in neat corduroy.

"I don't know how you feel about it, Sven," he said, "but I've no taste for the muck and moil in the July sun. There are a few thousands yet in the gravel pile and our friend here appears to be a willing worker. Aren't you, son?"

Sven grunted and lowered the end of the Winchester to the ground. It looked like a small stick in his hand, and the big pistol which girded him was a toy against the hugeness of his thigh.

"Don't let us interrupt your work, my friend," said the young man.

"How did you make it across the sinks?" said Tim.

"Why, as to that, there are two men who didn't—two men and a mule." He laughed quietly and looked at his gun.

Tim saw the extra canteen which was slung about Sven, and knew with an abrupt insight why the two were not here.

"A pleasant place," said the young man. "I dare say that you have had all this peak with its foothills to yourself. Looks like there is game. I told you there would be game, Sven. Something to eat. Something to kill."

"You vant Aye should shoot some meat, Mr. Bonnet? Or you vant to hunt it again?"

"Seen any mountain lion or bear up here, my young friend?"

Tim looked from Bonnet to Sven. Something of the terror of his situation was coming clear to him, turning his stomach like ground glass.

"Our young friend here doesn't seem to be of much help as a hunting guide. Supposing you step out there, Sven, and take a bead on a potential banquet. If you see any bear or puma, or anything worthwhile, let me know."

Bonnet did not bother to aim a weapon. He had already possessed himself of the rifle that had been in Tim's camp and had loaded it. He let it lie unnoticed at his feet.

Tim looked at the rifle and at the far bank. A crooked, almost hopeful smile appeared faintly on Bonnet's face. He hitched himself back a few feet from the rifle. His tongue caressed his parched lips. Tim was cold inside. Bonnet hitched himself further away from the weapon, and his smile grew, showing even, perfect teeth.

Bonnet reached inside his coat and brought out a short gun which he tossed down the bank so that it lay only a little further from Tim than the rifle was from Bonnet.

Tim's fingernails were sinking into the sluice. He could envision himself lunging forward and grabbing the gun, could see Bonnet snatching at the rifle. He tried desperately to anticipate the outcome, crouched a little lower.

Suddenly Tim sprang up the bank, sweeping the Smith and Wesson into his grasp and leveling it. With some astonishment he saw that Bonnet had not moved but stood looking with bright eyes upon Tim. The Smith and Wesson's hammer fell on an empty chamber, then another—another, another, another and another.

Bonnet picked up the rifle, jacked the shell into its chamber and laid the weapon across his knees. "Throw the gun here, young man. In a few days, when you have all the gold out of that gravel and neatly sacked, you and I may yet entertain ourselves with a little sport." He laughed quietly.

To find out more about *Devil's Manhunt* and how you can obtain your copy, go to www.goldenagestories.com.

Glossary

STORIES FROM THE GOLDEN AGE *reflect the words and expressions used in the 1930s and 1940s, adding unique flavor and authenticity to the tales. While a character's speech may often reflect regional origins, it also can convey attitudes common in the day. So that readers can better grasp such cultural and historical terms, uncommon words or expressions of the era, the following glossary has been provided.*

---

applehorn: style of saddle so named from the small horn whose top was round like an apple, compared to the broad, flat horns of saddles it replaced.

batwings: long chaps (leather leggings the cowboy wears to protect his legs) with big flaps of leather. They usually fasten with rings and snaps.

bead on, take a: to take careful aim at. This term alludes to the *bead*, a small metal knob on a firearm used as a front sight.

belly robber: a name often given to the cook, especially if he was a poor one.

bonnet strings: buckskin thongs hanging from each side of the brim of a cowman's hat at its inner edges. The ends are run through a bead or ring, and by pulling these up under the chin, the cowboy has a hat that will stay on during a fast ride or windy weather.

Bull: Bull Durham brand of tobacco.

cantle: the raised back part of a saddle for a horse.

cayuse: used by the northern cowboy in referring to any horse. At first the term was used for the Western horse to set it apart from a horse brought overland from the East. Later the name was applied as a term of contempt to any scrubby, undersized horse. Named after the Cayuse Indian tribe.

chuck wagon: a mess wagon of the cow country. It is usually made by fitting, at the back end of an ordinary farm wagon, a large box that contains shelves and has a hinged lid fitted with legs that serves as a table when lowered. The chuck wagon is a cowboy's home on the range, where he keeps his bedroll and dry clothes, gets his food and has a warm fire.

circuit court: a court that moves from place to place within a particular judicial district.

Colt: a single-action, six-shot cylinder revolver, most commonly available in .45- or .44-caliber versions. It was first manufactured in 1873 for the Army by the Colt Firearms Company, the armory founded by American inventor Samuel Colt (1814–1862) who revolutionized the firearms industry with the invention of the revolver. The Colt, also known as the Peacemaker, was also made available to civilians. As a reliable, inexpensive and popular handgun among cowboys, it became known as the "cowboy's gun" and a symbol of the Old West.

concentrate: the desired mineral that is left after impurities have been removed from mined ore.

coulee: a deep ravine or gulch, usually dry, that has been formed by running water.

crosstrees: on a pack saddle, the crossed pieces of wood connected to the front and back parts of the saddle. Crosstrees were used to distribute the pressure and load more evenly upon the animal, providing greater comfort.

cyanide mining: a highly toxic method of extracting gold and other metals from raw ore. Cyanide is applied to the ore, where it bonds with microscopic flecks of gold which are then recovered from the cyanide solution.

Derringer: a pocket-sized, short-barreled, large-caliber pistol. Named for the US gunsmith Henry Deringer (1786–1868), who designed it.

diamond hitch: a hitch is a kind of knot used to fasten one thing temporarily to another. The diamond hitch is a common method of roping a pack on an animal. It keeps the cargo from moving in any direction by holding it on the animal's back and when completed, the rope forms the figure of a diamond on top of the pack.

double-bitted ax: an ax that has cutting edges on both sides of the head.

drew rein: from "draw in the reins," meaning to slow down or stop by exerting pressure on the reins.

drifts: horizontal (or nearly horizontal) passageways in a mine.

dry-gulch: to kill; ambush.

false-front: describes a façade falsifying the size, finish or importance of a building.

faro: a gambling game played with cards and popular in the American West of the nineteenth century. In faro, the players bet on the order in which the cards will be turned over by the dealer. The cards were kept in a dealing box to keep track of the play.

feeder: from "feeder line," a branch of a main transportation line, as of a railroad.

G-men: government men; agents of the Federal Bureau of Investigation.

hardtack: a hard saltless biscuit.

Henry: the first rifle to use a cartridge with a metallic casing rather than the undependable, self-contained powder, ball and primer of previous rifles. It was named after B. Tyler Henry, who designed the rifle and the cartridge.

hog leg: another name for the popular Colt revolver also known as the Peacemaker.

hoss: horse.

hostler: a person who takes care of horses, especially at an inn.

jingle bobs: little pear-shaped pendants hanging loosely from the end of a spur (small spiked wheel attached to the heel of a rider's boot); their sole function is to make music.

larruping: beating or flogging.

livery stable: a stable that accommodates and looks after horses for their owners.

lode: a deposit of ore that fills a fissure in a rock, or a vein of ore deposited between layers of rock.

neck-reined: guided a horse by pressure of the reins against its neck.

Peacemaker: nickname for the single-action (that is, cocked by hand for each shot), six-shot Army model revolver first produced in 1873 by the Colt Firearms Company, the armory founded by Samuel Colt (1814–1862). The handgun of the Old West, it became the instrument of both lawmaker and lawbreaker during the last twenty-five years of the nineteenth century. It soon earned various names, such as "hog leg," "Equalizer," and "Judge Colt and his jury of six."

pill-throwers: gunmen; lead slingers.

pink tea: formal tea, reception or other social gathering usually attended by politicians, military officials and the like.

pinwheel: a movement or trick with a gun; the gun is held in virtual firing position except that the forefinger is not in the trigger guard. The gun is flipped into the air so that it revolves and the butt drops naturally into the palm of the hand.

puncher: a hired hand who tends cattle and performs other duties on horseback.

quartz: a common, hard mineral, often with brilliant crystals. It is generally found in large masses or veins, and mined for its gold content.

quirt: a riding whip with a short handle and a braided leather lash.

raked: slanted away from an upright position.

ramrod: a rod used for ramming down the charge in a gun that is loaded through the muzzle.

rannies: ranahans; cowboys or top ranch hands.

redeye: cheap, strong whiskey.

rein in: stop or slow one's horse by pulling on the reins.

remuda: a group of saddle horses from which ranch hands pick mounts for the day.

riata: a long noosed rope used to catch animals.

rifled: stolen; taken by force.

road agents: stagecoach robbers in the mid- to late-nineteenth-century American West.

rotgut: raw, inferior liquor.

run-over: of boots, where the heel is so unevenly worn on the outside that the back of the boot starts to lean to one side and does not sit straight above the heel.

scatter-gun: a cowboy's name for a shotgun.

Scheherazade: the female narrator of *The Arabian Nights,* who during one thousand and one adventurous nights saved her life by entertaining her husband, the king, with stories.

scorchers: branding irons.

shaver: a young boy.

single-action Army: Colt Single Action Army (SAA); a single-action, .45-caliber revolver holding six rounds. It was first manufactured in 1873 by the Colt Firearms Company, the armory founded by Samuel Colt (1814–1862). Initially produced for the Army to incorporate the latest metallic-cartridge technology, civilian versions were also made available in .32-, .38-, .41- and .44-calibers, among many others. The SAA, also referred to simply as Colt or the Peacemaker, gained popularity throughout the West and has become known as the "cowboy's gun."

Sioux shield: a shield of the Sioux (Indian people of North America). The shield was used for physical and spiritual protection. It was circular in shape and approximately eighteen inches in diameter.

sluice: sluice box; a long, narrow wood or metal artificial channel that water passes through when put in a creek or stream to separate the dirt and junk material away from the gold. Gold, a very dense metal, stays in the sluice box because of its heavy weight.

sombrero: a Mexican style of hat that was common in the Southwest. It had a high-curved wide brim, a long, loose chin strap and the crown was dented at the top. Like cowboy hats generally, it kept off the sun and rain, fended off the branches and served as a handy bucket or cup.

sougans: bedrolls; blankets or quilts with a protective canvas tarp for use on a bunk or on the range.

sowbelly: salt pork; pork cured in salt, especially fatty pork from the back, side or belly of a hog.

spittoon: a container for spitting into.

stamp mill: a machine that crushes ore.

tongue: the pole extending from a carriage or other vehicle between the animals drawing it.

Wellington boots: a boot worn and popularized by Arthur Wellesley, First Duke of Wellington and fashionable among the British aristocracy in the early nineteenth century. The First Duke had instructed his London shoemaker to modify the eighteenth-century Hessian boot (the standard issue footwear for the military, especially officers). The resulting new boot designed in soft calfskin leather had the trim removed and was cut closer around the leg. The heels were low cut, stacked around an inch, and the boot stopped at mid-calf.

West Point: US Military Academy in New York. It has been a military post since 1778 and the seat of the US Military Academy since 1802.

whitewash: a white liquid that is a mixture of lime or powdered chalk and water, used for making walls or ceilings white.

Winchester: an early family of repeating rifles; a single-barreled rifle containing multiple rounds of ammunition. Manufactured by the Winchester Repeating Arms Company, it was widely used in the US during the latter half of the nineteenth century. The 1873 model is often called "the gun that won the West" for its immense popularity at that time, as well as its use in fictional Westerns.

wind devil: a spinning column of air that moves across the landscape and picks up loose dust. It looks like a miniature tornado but is not as powerful.

L. Ron Hubbard
in the Golden Age
of Pulp Fiction

*In writing an adventure story
a writer has to know that he is adventuring
for a lot of people who cannot.
The writer has to take them here and there
about the globe and show them
excitement and love and realism.
As long as that writer is living the part of an
adventurer when he is hammering
the keys, he is succeeding with his story.*

*Adventuring is a state of mind.
If you adventure through life, you have a
good chance to be a success on paper.*

*Adventure doesn't mean globe-trotting,
exactly, and it doesn't mean great deeds.
Adventuring is like art.
You have to live it to make it real.*

—*L. RON HUBBARD*

L. Ron Hubbard
and American
Pulp Fiction

B ORN March 13, 1911, L. Ron Hubbard lived a life at
least as expansive as the stories with which he enthralled
a hundred million readers through a fifty-year career.

Originally hailing from Tilden, Nebraska, he spent his
formative years in a classically rugged Montana, replete with
the cowpunchers, lawmen and desperadoes who would later
people his Wild West adventures. And lest anyone imagine
those adventures were drawn from vicarious experience, he
was not only breaking broncs at a tender age, he was also
among the few whites ever admitted into Blackfoot society
as a bona fide blood brother. While if only to round out an
otherwise rough and tumble youth, his mother was that rarity
of her time—a thoroughly educated woman—who introduced
her son to the classics of Occidental literature even before
his seventh birthday.

But as any dedicated L. Ron Hubbard reader will attest, his
world extended far beyond Montana. In point of fact, and as the
son of a United States naval officer, by the age of eighteen he
had traveled over a quarter of a million miles. Included therein
were three Pacific crossings to a then still mysterious Asia, where
he ran with the likes of Her British Majesty's agent-in-place

L. Ron Hubbard, left, at Congressional Airport, Washington, DC, 1931, with members of George Washington University flying club.

for North China, and the last in the line of Royal Magicians from the court of Kublai Khan. For the record, L. Ron Hubbard was also among the first Westerners to gain admittance to forbidden Tibetan monasteries below Manchuria, and his photographs of China's Great Wall long graced American geography texts.

Upon his return to the United States and a hasty completion of his interrupted high school education, the young Ron Hubbard entered George Washington University. There, as fans of his aerial adventures may have heard, he earned his wings as a pioneering barnstormer at the dawn of American aviation. He also earned a place in free-flight record books for the longest sustained flight above Chicago. Moreover, as a roving reporter for *Sportsman Pilot* (featuring his first professionally penned articles), he further helped inspire a generation of pilots who would take America to world airpower.

Immediately beyond his sophomore year, Ron embarked on the first of his famed ethnological expeditions, initially to then untrammeled Caribbean shores (descriptions of which would later fill a whole series of West Indies mystery-thrillers). That the Puerto Rican interior would also figure into the future of Ron Hubbard stories was likewise no accident. For in addition to cultural studies of the island, a 1932–33

LRH expedition is rightly remembered as conducting the first complete mineralogical survey of a Puerto Rico under United States jurisdiction.

There was many another adventure along this vein: As a lifetime member of the famed Explorers Club, L. Ron Hubbard charted North Pacific waters with the first shipboard radio direction finder, and so pioneered a long-range navigation system universally employed until the late twentieth century. While not to put too fine an edge on it, he also held a rare Master Mariner's license to pilot any vessel, of any tonnage in any ocean.

Yet lest we stray too far afield, there is an LRH note at this juncture in his saga, and it reads in part:

"I started out writing for the pulps, writing the best I knew, writing for every mag on the stands, slanting as well as I could."

To which one might add: His earliest submissions date from the summer of 1934, and included tales drawn from true-to-life Asian adventures, with characters roughly modeled on British/American intelligence operatives he had known in Shanghai. His early Westerns were similarly peppered with details drawn from personal experience. Although therein lay a first hard lesson from the often cruel world of the pulps. His first Westerns were soundly rejected as lacking the authenticity of a Max Brand yarn

Capt. L. Ron Hubbard in Ketchikan, Alaska, 1940, on his Alaskan Radio Experimental Expedition, the first of three voyages conducted under the Explorers Club flag.

(a particularly frustrating comment given L. Ron Hubbard's Westerns came straight from his Montana homeland, while Max Brand was a mediocre New York poet named Frederick Schiller Faust, who turned out implausible six-shooter tales from the terrace of an Italian villa).

Nevertheless, and needless to say, L. Ron Hubbard persevered and soon earned a reputation as among the most publishable names in pulp fiction, with a ninety percent placement rate of first-draft manuscripts. He was also among the most prolific, averaging between seventy and a hundred thousand words a month. Hence the rumors that L. Ron Hubbard had redesigned a typewriter for faster keyboard action and pounded out manuscripts on a continuous roll of butcher paper to save the precious seconds it took to insert a single sheet of paper into manual typewriters of the day.

That all L. Ron Hubbard stories did not run beneath said byline is yet another aspect of pulp fiction lore. That is, as publishers periodically rejected manuscripts from top-drawer authors if only to avoid paying top dollar, L. Ron Hubbard and company just as frequently replied with submissions under various pseudonyms. In Ron's case, the

A MAN OF MANY NAMES

Between 1934 and 1950, L. Ron Hubbard authored more than fifteen million words of fiction in more than two hundred classic publications. To supply his fans and editors with stories across an array of genres and pulp titles, he adopted fifteen pseudonyms in addition to his already renowned L. Ron Hubbard byline.

Winchester Remington Colt
Lt. Jonathan Daly
Capt. Charles Gordon
Capt. L. Ron Hubbard
Bernard Hubbel
Michael Keith
Rene Lafayette
Legionnaire 148
Legionnaire 14830
Ken Martin
Scott Morgan
Lt. Scott Morgan
Kurt von Rachen
Barry Randolph
Capt. Humbert Reynolds

list included: Rene Lafayette, Captain Charles Gordon, Lt. Scott Morgan and the notorious Kurt von Rachen—supposedly on the lam for a murder rap, while hammering out two-fisted prose in Argentina. The point: While L. Ron Hubbard as Ken Martin spun stories of Southeast Asian intrigue, LRH as Barry Randolph authored tales of romance on the Western range—which, stretching between a dozen genres is how he came to stand among the two hundred elite authors providing close to a million tales through the glory days of American Pulp Fiction.

L. Ron Hubbard, circa 1930, at the outset of a literary career that would finally span half a century.

In evidence of exactly that, by 1936 L. Ron Hubbard was literally leading pulp fiction's elite as president of New York's American Fiction Guild. Members included a veritable pulp hall of fame: Lester "Doc Savage" Dent, Walter "The Shadow" Gibson, and the legendary Dashiell Hammett—to cite but a few.

Also in evidence of just where L. Ron Hubbard stood within his first two years on the American pulp circuit: By the spring of 1937, he was ensconced in Hollywood, adopting a Caribbean thriller for Columbia Pictures, remembered today as *The Secret of Treasure Island*. Comprising fifteen thirty-minute episodes, the L. Ron Hubbard screenplay led to the most profitable matinée serial in Hollywood history. In accord with Hollywood culture, he was thereafter continually called upon

The 1937 Secret of Treasure Island, *a fifteen-episode serial adapted for the screen by L. Ron Hubbard from his novel,* Murder at Pirate Castle.

to rewrite/doctor scripts—most famously for long-time friend and fellow adventurer Clark Gable.

In the interim—and herein lies another distinctive chapter of the L. Ron Hubbard story—he continually worked to open Pulp Kingdom gates to up-and-coming authors. Or, for that matter, anyone who wished to write. It was a fairly unconventional stance, as markets were already thin and competition razor sharp. But the fact remains, it was an L. Ron Hubbard hallmark that he vehemently lobbied on behalf of young authors—regularly supplying instructional articles to trade journals, guest-lecturing to short story classes at George Washington University and Harvard, and even founding his own creative writing competition. It was established in 1940, dubbed the Golden Pen, and guaranteed winners both New York representation and publication in *Argosy*.

But it was John W. Campbell Jr.'s *Astounding Science Fiction* that finally proved the most memorable LRH vehicle. While every fan of L. Ron Hubbard's galactic epics undoubtedly knows the story, it nonetheless bears repeating: By late 1938, the pulp publishing magnate of Street & Smith was determined to revamp *Astounding Science Fiction* for broader readership. In particular, senior editorial director F. Orlin Tremaine called for stories with a stronger *human element*. When acting editor John W. Campbell balked, preferring his spaceship-driven tales, Tremaine enlisted Hubbard. Hubbard, in turn, replied with the genre's first truly *character-driven* works, wherein heroes are pitted not against bug-eyed monsters but the mystery and majesty of deep space itself—and thus was launched the Golden Age of Science Fiction.

The names alone are enough to quicken the pulse of any science fiction aficionado, including LRH friend and protégé, Robert Heinlein, Isaac Asimov, A. E. van Vogt and Ray Bradbury. Moreover, when coupled with LRH stories of fantasy, we further come to what's rightly been described as the foundation of every modern tale of horror: L. Ron Hubbard's immortal *Fear.* It was rightly proclaimed by Stephen King as one of the very few works to genuinely warrant that overworked term "classic"—as in: *"This is a classic tale of creeping, surreal menace and horror. . . . This is one of the really, really good ones."*

L. Ron Hubbard, 1948, among fellow science fiction luminaries at the World Science Fiction Convention in Toronto.

To accommodate the greater body of L. Ron Hubbard fantasies, Street & Smith inaugurated *Unknown*—a classic pulp if there ever was one, and wherein readers were soon thrilling to the likes of *Typewriter in the Sky* and *Slaves of Sleep* of which Frederik Pohl would declare: *"There are bits and pieces from Ron's work that became part of the language in ways that very few other writers managed."*

And, indeed, at J. W. Campbell Jr.'s insistence, Ron was regularly drawing on themes from the Arabian Nights and so introducing readers to a world of genies, jinn, Aladdin and Sinbad—all of which, of course, continue to float through cultural mythology to this day.

At least as influential in terms of post-apocalypse stories was L. Ron Hubbard's 1940 *Final Blackout*. Generally acclaimed as the finest anti-war novel of the decade and among the ten best works of the genre ever authored—here, too, was a tale that would live on in ways few other writers imagined.

Portland, Oregon, 1943; L. Ron Hubbard, captain of the US Navy subchaser PC 815.

Hence, the later Robert Heinlein verdict: "Final Blackout *is as perfect a piece of science fiction as has ever been written."*

Like many another who both lived and wrote American pulp adventure, the war proved a tragic end to Ron's sojourn in the pulps. He served with distinction in four theaters and was highly decorated for commanding corvettes in the North Pacific. He was also grievously wounded in combat, lost many a close friend and colleague and thus resolved to say farewell to pulp fiction and devote himself to what it had supported these many years—namely, his serious research.

But in no way was the LRH literary saga at an end, for as he wrote some thirty years later, in 1980:

"Recently there came a period when I had little to do. This was novel in a life so crammed with busy years, and I decided to amuse myself by writing a novel that was pure *science fiction."*

That work was *Battlefield Earth: A Saga of the Year 3000*. It was an immediate *New York Times* bestseller and, in fact, the first international science fiction blockbuster in decades. It was not, however, L. Ron Hubbard's magnum opus, as that distinction is generally reserved for his next and final work: The 1.2 million word *Mission Earth*.

> **Final Blackout**
> *is as perfect
> a piece of
> science fiction
> as has ever
> been written.*
>
> —Robert Heinlein

How he managed those 1.2 million words in just over twelve months is yet another piece of the L. Ron Hubbard legend. But the fact remains, he did indeed author a ten-volume *dekalogy* that lives in publishing history for the fact that each and every volume of the series was also a *New York Times* bestseller.

Moreover, as subsequent generations discovered L. Ron Hubbard through republished works and novelizations of his screenplays, the mere fact of his name on a cover signaled an international bestseller. . . . Until, to date, sales of his works exceed hundreds of millions, and he otherwise remains among the most enduring and widely read authors in literary history. Although as a final word on the tales of L. Ron Hubbard, perhaps it's enough to simply reiterate what editors told readers in the glory days of American Pulp Fiction:

He writes the way he does, brothers, because he's been there, seen it and done it!

THE STORIES FROM THE
GOLDEN AGE

Your ticket to adventure starts here with the Stories from
the Golden Age collection by master storyteller L. Ron Hubbard.
These gripping tales are set in a kaleidoscope of exotic locales and brim
with fascinating characters, including some of the
most vile villains, dangerous dames and brazen heroes
you'll ever get to meet.

The entire collection of over one hundred and fifty stories is being
released in a series of eighty books and audiobooks.
For an up-to-date listing of available titles,
go to www.goldenagestories.com.

AIR ADVENTURE

FAR-FLUNG ADVENTURE

SEA ADVENTURE

TALES FROM THE ORIENT

The Devil—With Wings   *Pearl Pirate*
The Falcon Killer   *The Red Dragon*
Five Mex for a Million   *Spy Killer*
Golden Hell   *Tah*
The Green God   *The Trail of the Red Diamonds*
Hurricane's Roar   *Wind-Gone-Mad*
Inky Odds   *Yellow Loot*
Orders Is Orders

MYSTERY

The Blow Torch Murder   *The Grease Spot*
Brass Keys to Murder   *Killer Ape*
Calling Squad Cars!   *Killer's Law*
The Carnival of Death   *The Mad Dog Murder*
The Chee-Chalker   *Mouthpiece*
Dead Men Kill   *Murder Afloat*
The Death Flyer   *The Slickers*
Flame City   *They Killed Him Dead*

FANTASY

SCIENCE FICTION

WESTERN